THE RAVEN

THE RAVEN

A Come and Get Me Novel:
Book One

Shay Therese

Lake River Press
PO BOX 974
Ridgefield, WA 98642

Cover Design by Brittany Peru

The Raven
Copyright © 2023 by Shay Therese

ISBN: 979-8-9894426-0-7

To the women!

To Ashley, Brittany, Denise, Kelly, Stephanie.

To my mom and sisters.

To the Ravens of the world who never stopped fighting.

To all the Lost Birds. May you find your way back home.

Prologue

1987, Rain Tree Indian Reservation, WI, USA

Lena Winters: Can you tell me the one about Raven again?

Darren Winters: The one with Black Bear? Or Wolf?

Lena Winters: The one with Wolf. I love the way it starts.

Darren Winters: Hmm, how did that one start again...

Lena Winters: Daaad!

Darren Winters: Oh that's right, Wolf had always loved Raven...

Chapter One

The sound of creaking floorboards awoke me from a dreamless sleep. Rosie's soft growling from the foot of my bed sent the hair on my arms rising. Someone was in my house. My heart pounded in my chest as I lay still, listening, assessing. I could tell they were just outside my bedroom door. Rosie's quiet growl continued. I whispered to her, "It's okay, girl," even though it certainly was not.

I needed to get Rocky's gun from under the bed but was unsure of how to do it without making any noise. I was instantly filled with regret for having kept it in the small gun safe. *Is the combination still 1234? Shit, what if Rocky changed it and never told me the new code? Is it even loaded? Cocked? Would I have to cock it?* He had only shown it to me once. Unfortunately, my time to contemplate was over as I heard the soft clicking of the inner workings of the door's handle.

I had to make my move.

I flung myself toward the ground right as the door opened, and Rosie leaped off the bed. Vicious barks, snarls, and the sounds of a struggle proceeded. *Damn it!* I couldn't move. My legs were tangled in the top sheet and my lower body was awkwardly still half on the mattress as I reached beneath the bed, clawing for the safe.

An angry slur of profanity came from a deep, gruff voice, utterly terrifying me. *Had Rosie got to him?*

There! My fingers made contact with cold metal, stinging them, but then I heard Rosie's heartbreaking whimper followed by a loud thud. My stomach lurched, and I screamed Rosie's name as I pressed four buttons down a straight line. *Quicker! I needed to be quicker!* Upside down and in the dark, I had no idea which button was number one versus number four on the small safe.

"Fucking dog. Serves you right," said the voice as a solid red light from the safe flashed before my eyes. *Shit!* I jerked the rest of my body off the bed, landing hard on my side, the top sheet untucking and coming with me, along with my comforter. I quickly pushed the four buttons again but in the other direction this time. A split second later, a pale-green light flashed, and I heard a quiet click.

I raised my head toward the man now standing in my direct line of sight. The low light streaming in from the hallway allowed me to just make out his features, he seemed to be staring back at me with a hunger that made my insides turn.

"Don't worry, you'll be with your little bitch dog, soon enough. I'll give you that at least," he snarled down at me.

With my hands concealed under the bed, I grabbed the small handgun, sliding it under my comforter toward my body. The man took a step, moving closer to me, and at that moment, I saw a large knife in his hand, glinting in the darkness. My chest heaving, I turned swiftly so I was upright, my bare butt now flush on the cold hardwood floor.

"*Fuck you*!" I screamed and pulled the trigger. The blow caused my body to thrust back against my nightstand.

A masculine wail escaped the bastard as he fell back against the wall opposite me and slid to the ground. A clink on the floor made me believe he was now knifeless, but on the ground and in the dark, I couldn't be sure. A terrible thought crossed my mind that he might have another weapon. I frantically untangled my trapped legs from the top sheet and got to my feet, leaning back slightly. My eyes never moved away from him as I reached my arm back to fumble with the lamp and flicked on the light.

I was distantly aware of the strange stench permeating off the man now slouched down on himself in front of me. He smelled of stale shit and urine—not that I knew exactly what stale shit smelled like, but I imagined it smelled like him. He appeared to be no stranger to the bottle either, his hair greasy and his eyes glassy.

"You bitch. You *fucking bitch*! You shot me! I only wanted to play," he cried out, utter shock on his plain, pale face.

I stood before him fully naked, as that is how I slept most nights— but now never would again. I had shot him. It had been loaded and cocked! *Thank you, Rocky!* One last gift from my love.

I took notice that his knife was just out of arm's reach, close to Rosie. Her body was limp, and she wasn't moving. Panic and something else flared inside me. "You killed my dog! You killed my baby!" I stared at him as an icy cold washed over me, not because I was naked and not because it was a frigid night in November in Green Bay.

No, the cold that flitted through me was none other than pure and absolute ruthlessness. I knew exactly what I was going to do. There was nothing I'd been more sure of in my entire life. "I'm going to kill you, you piece of shit. You know that, right?"

He clutched his stomach as blood seeped out of him. An awful lot of blood, too. The man looked up at me, his scraggly hair falling into his dark eyes. He disgusted me.

He moaned and rolled a little to sit up straighter against the wall, but he didn't beg. He didn't beg or say sorry or anything. For some reason, I expected an apology. Though, did I want him to give me a reason not to kill him? No, certainly not. So I moved a step closer, thinking about what he was doing in my house, thinking about what he may have done to other women.

"What were you going to do? Rape me and then kill me? Do some sick, weird shit?" He didn't answer, so I continued, "You look the type who would, you sick fuck."

He glared at me. "Oh, and so much more," he said through clenched teeth. He coughed a small pitiful cough, still clutching his stomach. Then he leered at my naked body and licked his lips in a suggestive manner.

I moved my outstretched arm, aimed the gun at his crotch, and just as I could see his eyes bulge and his mouth starting to form words surely of protest, I pulled the trigger. This time, my stance made the blow less shocking. He made a choking sound before releasing a sob and scream; a pained sound so horrible that I wanted to cover my ears. But I didn't. Instead, I stood there watching him bleeding and crying, unsure of what to do next.

He wasn't dead. I didn't own a cell phone anymore or have a landline. I could probably contact authorities from my laptop, but it was in my office and there was no way I could walk away from him while he was still breathing. He was still too dangerous.

He was cussing and whimpering, now on his side, and he was very close to where the knife laid—too close. I kept my aim at him and hoped there were more bullets in the gun. Rocky had never shot it as far as I knew, so it should have been fully loaded. *How many bullets are in a gun, anyway?*

"Put the gun down!" A man in police attire was standing in my bedroom doorway aiming a gun at me.

How had I not heard any sirens or my front door being opened? Though, I heard them then; sirens and movements outside my bedroom.

I made eye contact with the officer, and for a second, I almost did put the gun down. But movement out of the corner of my eye made both of us look toward the bleeding, groaning, wretched excuse of a man on my floor. He had grabbed the knife and was moving his arm back to fling it toward me.

And that was all I needed; I fired again.

The knife dropped from his slackened hand, and his body slumped. His eyes stared blankly at me, but at the same time, stared at nothing. Nothing at all.

I stepped backward and bumped into my nightstand, lowering the gun slowly to my side. The police officer who'd ordered me to put down my gun moved around Rosie and the now dead man, and over to me.

He was speaking to me, but I wasn't hearing him. I was staring at the man I'd just killed. The man I'd shot three times.

Slowly, the officer's voice penetrated the fog. "Miss, it's going to be okay. Give me the gun. You're going to be okay." I looked up at him. "Give me the gun," he repeated.

He had kind, blue eyes.

Chapter Two

There were others in the room. I could hear them moving around, but I didn't see them. All I saw was the blue-eyed man in front of me, his body blocking the rest of the happenings. Slowly, I set Rocky's gun on the bed instead of his outstretched hand. He grabbed it quickly and handed it back to someone else.

The shock of what had just happened hit me like a train, and my body started to shake uncontrollably. "M-m-my, m-my dog. He…he brr-broke into my h-house. Sh-she saved m-me." My teeth were chattering so hard, but I couldn't stop it.

The officer grabbed my comforter off the floor and wrapped it around me, holding the edges together in front of me. My hands tried to grasp the blanket, but they felt numb, and I couldn't keep the edges held together.

"I've got you. You're going to be okay. I'm Officer Rivers. What's your name?" He moved his head to the side and shouted, "Salone, get someone to check on the dog and grab this woman some clothes."

Oh, right, I was naked. I stumbled, my legs almost giving out, but then the officer's arms were around me, holding me up.

"Nnn-name's Raven. Please d-d-don't let g-go." I don't know why I said it, but I needed to be held. Not just to be kept upright, but for comfort, which was not something I wanted to admit. He slowly brought me to him, careful of his gear, wrapping his arms around me and keeping me tight against his body. My shaking continued.

"Raven, are you hurt? Did he hurt you at all?"

I shook my head as tremors went through me. "Nnn-no." Fuck, my teeth wouldn't stop chattering. "He d-didn't get the ch-chance."

"This brave pup has a pulse! A lot of blood loss, but we can't take her in the ambulance. Can somebody get her to BluePearl?" yelled someone kneeling by Rosie, holding a large white gauze pad to her side. I let out a breath at the news Rosie was alive, and my legs buckled under me, but the officer held me up and guided me to the bed to sit, his warm arms still wrapped around me, holding the comforter securely.

We sat there together while my shaking slowly subsided. He asked me simple questions about who I was: my age, if I lived alone, when I moved here, my dog's name—all while assuring me everything was going to be okay. I quietly answered the questions: 28; yes, I lived alone; I moved here about a year ago; her name is Rosie. Whether or not it was smart for me to answer questions right now didn't matter to me; I was just thankful to know that for the moment, Rosie still had a fighting chance.

Eventually, another officer appeared in front of us. She was older, probably in her sixties, short, with spikey cropped white hair and deep creases on her forehead and around her eyes. She held a pile of my clothes in her arms. "Hi, Miss Lowe? Is that your name, Raven Lowe?" I nodded. "I'm Officer Salone. I bet you want to get the hell out of this room and into some clothes. Officer Rivers is going to walk you to your bathroom so you can get dressed. Alright?"

I nodded again.

Officer Rivers and I rose together off the bed. His body was tall, and he angled himself to my other side to block the bloody sight on the floor from my vision, purposefully, I realized—so I didn't have to see what I had done.

"Just keep your eyes on me," he said, his voice calm. And so, I did—until we reached where Rosie was. She was still being tended to, caressed carefully by an emergency medical staff person. I wanted to go to my girl, to hug her and kiss her and tell her thank you, but

Officer Rivers was quickly and firmly ushering me away, and I knew if I turned back around, I'd have to see the man I had killed.

"You can call me Wolf." Officer Rivers' voice snapped me back to the present.

We had stopped in front of my bathroom, which was across from my bedroom door and a little to the right. I was thankful that if I turned around I couldn't see into my room. Officer Salone placed the clothes she had for me on the bathroom counter before walking out, and Officer Rivers eased his arm away from me. "Do you have a hold on it?" He motioned with his head to where he clasped the comforter.

"I've got it. Thank you." He released the blanket, and I walked into the bathroom and shut the door, locking it.

I stood there, my bare feet freezing on the tiled bathroom floor, and I stared into the mirror. I didn't recognize myself. My face was pale. *Pale.* I didn't even know it was possible for my skin to look pale. My stomach started to turn at the thought of what had just occurred, and I retched into the sink, my long black hair spilling into the bowl as I lurched forward. My hair was now covered in bile. *Wonderful. What a fucked-up night.*

I quickly rinsed the sink, my hair, and then my mouth out with water and brushed my teeth. When I moved toward the shower and turned the water on, I heard a light knock on the door. I ignored it. I couldn't care less what the officers thought or about police procedure at a time like this. I stepped into the tub, letting the icy cold water ravage my face and body into awareness as it gradually turned to warm, and then hot.

I had just killed someone.

A tremor went through my body at the thought. He had broken into my house with the intention of doing horrible things to me, and I'd stopped him. Well, my sweet girl had stopped him first. I wasn't a religious person, but I said a quick prayer to whomever would listen that Rosie would be alright.

I scrubbed my hair and every inch of my body. Three times I scrubbed myself. The man hadn't even gotten a hand on me, and yet I felt so incredibly violated. Anger rushed through me in agonizing waves. I was glad I'd killed that fucker. Glad he couldn't do what he had intended to anyone else ever again.

I washed and rinsed my hair one last time and turned the faucet off. I glanced out of the tub and stared at my white comforter on the floor. There was no blood on it. There was no blood on me. What kind of gun had Rocky bought, anyway? I didn't know a single thing about guns, but I thought maybe it would've been a bit messier than it had been, to shoot someone at such close range. I also figured the sound would've been louder, more painful to my ears. It hadn't been anything like in the movies.

I sighed and put on the clothes Officer Salone had picked out for me. A pair of dull, yellow-colored granny panties that I usually only wore when I was on my period, a thin white camisole, pajama bottoms with alternating types of kittens wearing Santa hats, and my newish Green Bay Packer sweatshirt. No bra and no socks. A real fashionista, this Salone. My hair was still damp from just a towel-dry, so I swooped it up into a loose bun.

Frozen at the door, I looked back at my reflection. Although some color had come back into my face, I still looked like I'd seen a ghost, which, honestly, I felt I'd seen something far worse. I had been face to face with what seemed like the epitome of evil. I shuddered at the realization of how close that evil had come to touching me. *That sick son of a bitch!*

I took a deep breath to ebb my rising anger as I grabbed the door handle. This night was going to be a long one. Flashbacks of the morning of Rocky's death and all the accompanying questions flooded my brain. I took one more deep breath and exited the bathroom.

Officer Salone and Officer Rivers were standing near my small kitchen table—a simple black rectangle with two matching black chairs on either side. The older officer looked less than impressed that I'd taken a shower.

Officer Rivers handed me a bottle of water as I approached them. He was tall, around six-foot-four if I had to guess, and although he was wearing a lot of gear and a jacket, he looked lean and fit. I locked on to his blue eyes like they were my only anchor to this whole crazy, fucked-up night. He smiled carefully at me with a kind and very handsome face. He had a straight sharp nose, full mouth, and a stubble of a beard under those sparkling eyes.

"Take small sips. It'll help," he said. Clearly, he'd heard me unleash the contents of my stomach.

"Thanks," I said, cracking the bottle open and taking a sip. I leaned back against my kitchen table opposite the two officers. People were still milling in and out of my home, but I tried to ignore it. I knew how this would go, and before I would allow myself to be peppered with questions, I needed to know about the body.

"Is he gone?" I looked at Officer Rivers, but Officer Salone responded first.

"Yes, Miss Lowe, the body is gone. Did you know him?"

And straight into the questioning we went. I sighed. "Just call me Raven, and no, I have never seen that man in my life."

It had been very dark until I'd turned my lamp on and, though it wasn't the brightest of lights, I was certain I'd never laid eyes on him before. Had he seen me before? Had he followed me home from the grocery store or post office earlier?

Officer Rivers saw my wheels turning and asked, "Is there any reason you can think of why he wanted to break in? Cause you harm?"

I shook my head. "Look, I was asleep in my own home when all of a sudden, I heard noises outside my bedroom and my dog growling.

The door to my room opened, and I instantly moved to grab the gun under my bed. Everything happened so fast—"

"Is that your gun?" Officer Salone cut in, her face stoic.

Annoyed I'd been cut off, I tried to keep my voice even as I answered, "No. It was my boyfriend's."

Officer Salone leaned forward slightly. "What is his name, and what do you mean it *was* his gun?"

I kept my composure as best I could and took a deep breath. "His name was Rocky Everson, and it was his gun before he died."

She straightened back up. "How did he die?"

I looked down at my bare feet as the burn of tears behind my eyes cautioned me of their appearance. I hadn't really let myself think about that morning much at all over the years, so when the memory threatened its ugly reality, I usually shut down. I couldn't do that in front of the questioning officer, though, so I squeezed my nails into my palms as I spoke in a clipped tone, "His heart. He had a heart condition that had gone undiagnosed. I woke up one morning and he was gone." I managed to say the unbearable, the unthinkable, the unimaginable, but unfortunately for Rocky and all of us who'd loved him, the truth.

The old bag wasn't satisfied, though. "And when was this?"

"Four years ago, this December." I looked up at her, now thoroughly irritated this night had turned into speaking about a memory I spent most days avoiding.

Officer Rivers grimaced slightly at Salone then looked me in the eyes. "We are sorry for your loss. Let's get you down to the station to get your full statement, and we'll go from there," he said.

"Alright," I uttered quietly before moving off the table to get my shoes. *Go from there* didn't sound promising; it sounded endless.

Chapter Three

Down at the "station," which ended up being the Green Bay Police Department, I had to give a full statement twice to two detectives. Multiple employees had come in and out of the small room I was being interviewed in, and I wasn't sure anymore who was who.

After not having seen Officers Salone or Rivers since we first arrived at the station, they both finally entered the room and informed me Rosie was at a nearby veterinarian emergency hospital and in stable condition, and I could check in on her tomorrow. I was overcome with gratitude that strangers had gotten her the help she'd needed and was about to say as much when one of the detectives still in the room slid me paper and pen to write my statement.

"Isn't what I said multiple times now recorded? Is it seriously necessary I write it down?" I managed to keep the childish whine out of my voice, but I was so, so over this night.

"Writing it down may help you remember some detail you forgot," the detective—O'Dell, I thought was his name—insisted. I looked up at Officer Rivers—Wolf, as he had told me to call him. Was that seriously his name? I supposed I wasn't one to judge with my name being of the animal variety as well.

The handsome officer looked as tired as I felt, his shorter blond hair mussed like he'd run his fingers through it a few times before coming in here. "It's true. Many times, writing it down can be helpful," he said thoughtfully.

I felt like I was back in elementary school being told to practice writing my spelling words.

"If you make a mistake, draw one simple line through the text and initial it," said the detective.

I grabbed the pen and started writing as the staff of the Green Bay Police Department exited the room, leaving me alone. I couldn't believe I was there. Never in my wildest dreams did I think I'd be in a police station writing down my statement about *killing* someone.

I wrote down, in sickening detail, everything I'd already said multiple times. And just as I had those times, I left out the time and conversation between shot number one and number two. I sat back in my chair and contemplated my actions of leaving out details.

I didn't know much about court proceedings, but I knew enough that my premeditated crotch shot would be an issue with a judge or jury. Or at least, I figured it would be if I were to have charges brought against me. So instead of telling the truth, I explained that after shot number one, I scrambled to my feet, and once I got my senses about me, I made out he was going to throw the knife and I shot at him again, obviously fearing for my life. I left out the detail about turning on the light until after shot number two. That way, I could blame my aim on the lack of light rather than the reality which had been intentional. I wasn't sure if my third and final shot would be an issue, but I couldn't lie about that one since the officer had witnessed it all. At least he could corroborate the man had truly gone for his knife. It had technically been self-defense.

Soon after I set down my pen and shoved the sheets of paper away, Officers Salone and Rivers came back into the room. I was sure someone had been watching me from wherever they had their monitors. The older woman took the paper and pen and told her counterpart she'd see him again in a few hours, and she'd give my written statement to Detective O'Dell before leaving. She gave me what, I assumed, was her best attempt at an encouraging look that seemed to say things would get better and left the room.

Then it was just me and the blue-eyed officer.

"Are you sure there isn't anything I can get for you?" he asked.

I'd been continuously offered food, coffee, soda (or pop, as they say in Green Bay), but I'd politely refused it all. There was no way I could stomach anything other than the bottle of water I had been given at my house, which was still halfway full. "Thanks, but I'm fine. Is this night almost over? Can I leave now, or am I being charged with anything?" I asked.

"No, you are not being charged with anything at this time. You should probably call someone to come pick you up. Do you have your phone with you?"

I stood up from the chair and looked at him. "I don't have a phone."

He stared at me, hands resting up on his vest. "Really? Did it break or something?" He moved to open the door.

"No, it didn't break. Some people just want to live in the moment and not be addicted to technology. Also, I meant no, I don't have anyone to call *and* there's no one to pick me up."

His tired blue eyes creased in an odd assessment, like he wanted to tell me that was weird—and he would, of course, be right. It was weird.

"Well, you are allowed to go back to your home. I just figured you'd want to stay somewhere else for the night."

I crossed my arms over my chest. He wasn't wrong. I definitely did not want to go back there tonight, especially without Rosie. "Can you just call me an Uber or Lyft to take me somewhere, and I'll give you cash for it?" I reached for my purse—the only other thing I'd grabbed before I'd left my house besides my shoes.

"You really don't have any friends, co-workers, family around here you can stay with for the evening?" he prodded, though, not unkindly. I shook my head, pursing my lips. When it was obvious I wasn't going to elaborate, he asked, "Where will you go if you don't go to your house?"

"A hotel, I guess," I said flatly.

He looked at me for a few moments, conflict apparent in his features. "Alright…well, my shift is nearly over. Just give me a minute, and I'll drop you off on my way out."

The offer threw me for a moment and I diverted my eyes from him before deciding. "I appreciate it, thank you."

I took a seat on the small couch in the room as he exited and checked the clock hanging on the wall. It was almost three in the morning, which meant I had been there for at least three hours. My feet tapped on the floor, and the connection of my shoes hitting the tile kept me in the present. The shock had finally worn off, but now I was filled with adrenaline and an urge to not think of what had just occurred. I needed to move, to go…anywhere.

Anxious to get out of there, I stood up quickly when Officer Rivers walked back into the room. He held the door open for me to leave, and we walked down the hall and out the front doors of the station. I followed him toward a parked, already running, black Ford F150. I figured he'd drive me in the police vehicle we'd driven to the station in, but it made sense he would be heading home after he dropped me off; it was ridiculously early in the morning.

As we walked to his truck, he angled his head toward me. "I'm sorry we didn't have you grab some more of your things."

It hadn't been their fault; they'd told me to grab what I needed, but I hadn't been in the right mind at the time to make decisions about what I needed to bring with me.

Still too numb to even care about belongings, I said, "Don't worry about it, it's fine. I don't need anything tonight anyway. Just some sleep."

He eyed me as if he knew there was no way I was going to find sleep after what happened.

The thought pissed me off. Not only had a stranger broken into my house, almost killed my dog, intended to do, surely, vile things to me, caused me to *kill* him, but now he was stealing sleep from me as well.

It wasn't fair. And I was so, so tired.

The officer reached out, as if he was going to touch me, but then pulled his hand back to his side. "Are you okay?" he asked. Clearly this Wolf guy, was perceptive. "Sorry, that was a dumb question. Of course you aren't."

I managed a slight head nod with an appreciative glance toward him.

"I'm fine, I just…don't really want to be alone." An awkward confession to say out loud, and if I'd had my wits about me, I wouldn't have voiced it at all. Especially in front of a stranger. My exhaustion was bringing out an exposed side of me I didn't like. But if I was being completely honest, I couldn't help but feel somewhat comfortable with this man already. I'd never expected a cop to be like him. He seemed like a decent person. He had been respectful the whole time.

When we were at his truck, he told me to hop in on the passenger side, and I was thankful I'd be warm soon. I went around the front end of the truck and opened the door, hoisting myself into the front seat. I was sure he was probably breaking some policy by allowing this, but I couldn't bring myself to question it at this point. He appeared so self-assured, and although he looked younger, he definitely wasn't some rookie. Judging by how he acted, I assumed he was in his thirties.

Officer Rivers closed his door and adjusted himself in his seat, and our breath went from little moisture puffs outside to invisible in the fully warmed-up vehicle. He clicked on the seat warmers, and without looking at me, he surprised me by saying, "You can stay at my place for the night if you want. I have space, and this way you won't be alone."

I couldn't resist a quick glance at his left ring finger. No ring. He could be the type to take it off for work, but there were no markings to show there should be one. He had to have a partner. There was no way this thirty-something, obviously successful, and extremely—and I mean *extremely*—good-looking dude was single.

"Why didn't you shoot me?" I blurted out.

"What?" He quickly looked at me, shocked by my candor.

"I'm brown. You walked in and saw me standing there with a gun. Why didn't you shoot me? You could have, and no one would have faulted you. In fact, no one would have cared." That last part was a little dramatic, but the truth, for the most part.

He looked at me for far too long of a moment and then calmly said, "I'm sorry if you've had bad experiences with police before. We aren't all bad. I didn't shoot you because I was assessing the situation, which is what I'm trained to do, and although you looked terrified, you seemed in control. Also, you weren't aiming at me." He smirked, trying to make light of such a serious subject.

Had I? Had I been in control? It didn't feel like "in control" was what I'd been in that moment. Something intense had flooded my body, but it wasn't control. No, more than control, what I had been, was determined. Determined to end that man's life. The realization made my heart start to beat faster.

I couldn't be left alone to my own thoughts tonight. I just couldn't be alone.

Officer Rivers put his truck in drive.

"Yes," I said quietly, looking out toward the passenger side window. "I'd like to stay at your place, please."

He didn't say anything as he drove on.

Chapter Four

We didn't talk during the ten-minute drive from the station to Wolf's house. My hair was now in a low ponytail, bound at the nape of my neck. I had pulled it forward to drape over my chest before pulling my sweatshirt hood up. I was now leaning against the window in an attempt to look like I was sleeping. While I didn't want to be alone, I did not want to talk.

As Wolf slowed our speed and turned into what looked like a decent neighborhood, I sat up straighter. I recognized it from my home-buying search over a year ago—the John Muir Park neighborhood. He probably had a Homeowners Association that made you keep your front lawn maintained or else you'd get annoying letters and eventually a fine. I always avoided places like that. I didn't like people in my business, and I especially didn't have any patience for some random person telling me what to do with my house or yard.

He pulled into the driveway of a white ranch-style home with a brick design which ran across the base, adding a small amount of character to an otherwise plain-looking home. He pushed a button on his driver's-side visor, and the two-car garage door lifted before he pulled in.

Inside his garage, it was very clean and organized. However, there was a stack of what looked like moving boxes taking up one whole side of the opposite wall and a large tool chest next to a long table that stretched the length of the back wall. A large fridge and freezer were near the door leading into his house.

When we went inside his home, a quick glance around told me something was a bit off. Not in a creepy way, but in a bare, almost non-lived-in way. Nothing was on the light-gray walls—no paintings, no pictures, no mirrors, nothing. The austerity continued as I followed him from the hall into the front room. A massive flat screen T.V. on the ground was plugged in, opposite from a gray couch against the other wall. The living room opened up into the dining area with a small walnut-colored kitchen table and four chairs. Around the corner was a surprisingly large kitchen. A quartz counter coming out from one wall with a single barstool separated the two rooms.

The entire house was so barren it almost made me sad to look at. My thoughts must have been obvious because Officer Rivers, taking off his coat, sounded a little embarrassed as he said, "Sorry, I moved in a few months ago and haven't had time to really unpack everything." He moved toward the kitchen and set his wallet and keys on the island.

I noticed his hand moving toward the gun on his belt and then changing direction toward his back pocket. As if he usually set his gun down along with his keys and wallet but thought better of it.

Thought better of it because of the killer now in his house.

Did he think I was a cold-blooded murderer? Did he doubt my story? How could he doubt me when I'd told the truth? Well, I had basically told the entire truth. My heart started racing, and I tried to calm myself down. He wouldn't have brought me back here with him if he thought I was capable of killing him.

He glanced around his kitchen a bit as if he was looking for something to do and when he failed to come up with anything he ran a hand through his hair. "I'm going to grab some clothes and then take a shower. You can sleep in my room, it's down the hall here," he pointed to the open doorway to the right of him. "I'll shower in the guest bathroom." He then opened the pantry door behind him and waved a hand. "Feel free to grab whatever food you want. I'm sure you're probably hungry. Oh, and the sheets on the bed are clean. The guest room doesn't have a bed yet, so I'll sleep on the couch. Sound good?"

I looked up at him, feeling a little awkward I was taking him away from his bed. "Thank you, Officer Rivers."

"Yeah, no problem. And please call me Wolf." His voice softened, "I'm very sorry for what happened to you tonight. Get some sleep. I can take you to check on your dog tomorrow."

My heart sped up even faster at the thought of my baby. My sweet girl who had bought me the time I'd needed to get the gun. She'd saved me.

I watched as Wolf filled up two glasses of water from his fridge and set one on the counter near me. "You good here?" Not being able to summon any words, I nodded in assurance. He picked up his glass but didn't make any move to leave the kitchen. "Alright, then. Well…goodnight, Raven." He lingered another moment before walking down the hall.

I stood in his kitchen, knowing I should take him up on his offer of food, but I still didn't have an appetite, and I was so incredibly drained.

I realized I'd been standing there for a while when I heard a door shut and water running. I walked down the hall and found his room. The bedroom was bare like the rest of the house, but the big bed, two side tables, and being alone reminded me too much of my own room at my own home, which was now tainted.

Was I ever going to be able to go back into my room again? Resentment found its way into my veins. Another thing that asshole had taken from me. I didn't even know his name! Didn't even ask anyone down at the station about it at all. The detectives must not have known his name either, telling me they'd be in touch if they had more questions. All I had been able to give them in the form of contact information was my email. I could tell the detectives, like Wolf, thought it was odd I didn't have a phone.

I sat down on his bed with the light and door still open. I could see down the hallway.

What if this psycho ruined everything? I had bought my house only a year ago after making my way to Green Bay. I liked it here. I liked being near the reservation, even if I wasn't going back and I didn't want to move again. Why was shit always so messed up? Could I not have any amount of normalcy in my life?

The sound of the shower turning off down the hall brought me out of my pity party. A few minutes later, Wolf came down the hallway in gray sweatpants and no shirt. I was right, he was fit. *Very* fit. He paused in the doorway, and I tried not to stare at the V-shaped muscle under his torso, or his chest, or his arms, for that matter.

"Are you alright?" He sighed at his poor choice of wording. "I mean, did you need something?"

Did I need something? I did, but I contemplated for a moment before deciding to tell him.

"I don't want to be alone in here. And I'm not saying that because I'm some weak-ass little girl who needs a big man to make her feel safe. I just…just can't be alone after what happened."

He looked at me and then at the bed, before reaching his decision. "Yeah. Of course. I can bring some blankets in here and sleep on the floor. And, for the record, I don't think you're weak for not wanting to be alone."

He turned to head out of the room, I assumed to grab more blankets, so I quickly said, "It's a big bed. The floor would make no sense, and it's too cold for that." Trying to keep it casual, I excused myself to the bathroom.

After using the bathroom and splashing some water on my face, I removed my sweatshirt and set it folded on the bathroom counter. I found some mouthwash and did a quick rinse. I came out in the white camisole, which basically was see through, and with it being so cold, my nipples were not helping any amount of subtlety I may have been going for. My breasts weren't huge by any means, but they were prominent on my small figure. But the man had already seen me naked and at my most vulnerable, which was probably why I didn't feel the urge to cross my arms in front of me. It was also probably why I somehow felt comfortable around him. A strange thing, after only knowing him for a few hours. There was an annoying sense of safety when I was near him. I hadn't felt that since Rocky, and before him, only when I was a small child during the Good Years, as I called them—the few short years I'd had with my adoptive parents.

Wolf was lying on the side of his bed closest to the door, on top of the covers with his arms behind his head, propped up on double pillows, but he sat up when he saw me. If he noticed my change from sweatshirt to basically topless, he didn't let on. The light was on. He looked so tired, and yet he'd kept the light on for me.

"I didn't know if you wanted to keep the light on or not. We can; I don't mind at all."

Before answering, I moved to the bed and slipped under the comforter and top sheet. I lasted maybe a second before panic flushed through my body and I sprang back up, stumbling out of the bed, almost falling, my heart pounding out of my chest.

The sheet! The fucking sheet that had wrapped around my legs. The feel of it had been like a restraint around my ankles, allowing no give. Flashes of what I'd gone through a few hours earlier went tumbling through my brain.

Wolf quickly leaped across the bed and came to stand beside me. "Raven?"

I pointed to the bed, my hand trembling. "The top sheet. I…I can't have it. I don't want it to touch me. Tonight, it…it got wrapped around my legs. Fuck! I'm going crazy!" I lifted my hands to my face. He placed his hands on either side of my arms. They were warm in contrast to my cool bareness and so big that his fingers were grazing the outer edges of my shoulder blades.

"You aren't going crazy. You just went through something traumatic and are having post-traumatic stress. It's unfortunately normal for this type of situation."

I knew he was right. I knew what was happening to me, and I knew I couldn't stop it. Having had my unfair share of trauma growing up, I knew how this would go. I just didn't know when and how it would appear. Clearly, top sheets were going to be an issue for me for the unforeseeable future, and that—well, that was a little upsetting to me. Anger was again at the forefront of my emotions. So much anger tonight, an emotion I didn't usually bear.

I pulled my hands away from my face and took a deep breath. Wolf let go of my arms and turned toward the bed. He grasped the top sheet, and with one solid yank, he ripped the entire sheet off his bed and walked out of the room with it.

Had he realized seeing it crumpled on the floor would have most likely set me off as well? Or was he just a clean freak and didn't want to make a mess? It was not only empty in his house but also pretty spotless. I hadn't seen any sign of a woman—or roommate, for that matter.

Clean freak, then.

I got in bed and lay on my back, staring up at the stagnant ceiling fan. I took deep breaths, in and out. I could do this. I could keep going. I could keep living after something like this. Killing someone was not going to define me. Especially some piece of shit who'd deserved it.

Wolf walked back in and hesitated near the light switch.

"You can turn the light off," I told him.

He flipped the switch, and a few seconds later, I felt him slide under the comforter. I turned my body away from him and squeezed my eyes shut. A tear threatened to leak out, and I realized I hadn't cried yet. Through this entire, horrible, crazy ordeal of a night, I hadn't cried. I had only screamed, cussed, killed, shaken, barfed, and gone mostly quiet.

Before I knew it was happening, my body started racking in sobs.

Tears flowed, and I muffled my cries in Wolf's comforter. I was about to tell him I was sorry—once I could manage words—but then his body was against mine. His warm, strong arms wrapped around me and pulled me into him.

His voice was kind, and deep, "It's going to be okay. You're safe."

I gripped onto this forearms, clinging to him tighter, hoping his hold would suffocate my body shakes.

He held me even closer. "I've got you. It's all going to be okay," his soft voice repeated.

And I wanted to believe him, even though I knew he was wrong. I knew things weren't going to be okay. Things had never been okay for me, not for any real length of time, anyway. But I was so tired, and I was so angry that I eventually let his soothing words and his warm, strong body calm me into oblivion.

Chapter Five

I vaguely remembered waking up at one point and screaming with panic, grabbing for Rosie only to find she wasn't there. Powerful hands clasped me, and Wolf's voice lulled me back to sleep. He was there. The police officer who hadn't shot me. The guy who had covered my naked body for me. He was with me. This man I had only known a short while but felt as if I'd known longer—much longer.

When I woke again, I was aware of three things: one, my head was on a smooth, muscular chest; two, I was drooling on said chest; and three, my eyes were crusted almost completely shut with dried tears.

A fucking mess.

My right arm was resting on his rib cage, and the contrast of our skin was so shocking I stared for a while with the one eye I was able to pry open; the other stayed sealed. My brown skin against his creamy, almost beige skin tone was alarming, to say the least. The previous partners I had found myself in a similar position with had not been white.

His chest rose and fell so calmly, so quietly that I was sure he was asleep. Soft, bright light seeped through the windows on either side of his bed. Even through the blinds, I could tell it was later in the morning. I lifted my hand off him and rose slowly away and off the bed. I snuck a quick, one-eyed glance at him before padding into the bathroom. He was…beautiful. He was fucking beautiful. He was all smooth skin and muscles. His breathing was soft, no snoring, and somehow it made him even hotter.

In the bathroom, I scrubbed my crusted-up eyes with water and rinsed my mouth again. It was very frigid in his house, so I grabbed my sweatshirt off the counter and put it on, then scooped my hair into a ponytail. I was going to see Rosie and hopefully figure out what the hell was going to happen next with the shitstorm that had just landed in my life.

When I quietly opened the bathroom door, I saw the bed was empty, and I heard a faucet running down the hall. He must've been getting ready in the other bathroom.

I got back into his bed and scooted to where he had been lying in the middle. It was still warm from his body. And damn it was cold, so cold in Wisconsin. The prior year, when I'd experienced my first fall here, I hadn't been able to sleep at night. I'd been positive there would be a homeless person freezing to death on the streets. I had driven around for hours a couple of nights in a row with blankets but hadn't seen anyone in need. I hadn't been sure where the homeless people went on cold nights, but they'd clearly had somewhere safe to go. The realization had allowed me to finally get some sleep.

After a few minutes, Wolf appeared in the doorway dressed in his police gear. He gave me a soft smile. I couldn't surmise if it was shy or just awkward, potentially doubting his decision on having invited some strange woman into his home.

He cleared his throat, "Good morning."

I sat up a little more. "Morning." I tried to return his smile and I most definitely knew mine bordered on awkward.

"Hey, so, I have to get to work. Um, but you know you can stay here or, I mean if you want, or…I can drop you off somewhere, uh," he stumbled over his words. "Yeah, but if you want to stay, I can come back to pick you up when I get word about seeing your pup."

Drop me off somewhere? We both knew at this point he was being polite since I had nowhere to go other than my now crime-scene home, which I definitely didn't want to go to. "I'll stay."

He looked a little relieved at that, his shoulders depressed just slightly. "Great, I mean, good. Eat whatever you want, and…um…you can order delivery of whatever. I put the iPad on my dresser for you." He pointed to the one tall dresser in the corner of his mostly empty room.

I felt like I should thank him for everything, but instead I just asked, "Is Wolf your real name?"

One side of his mouth quirked up. "Yeah. It's short for Wolfgang."

"Wolfgang Rivers? What a name."

He shrugged. "Wolfgang is a family name on my mom's side. I've just always gone by Wolf."

I tried to smile, but I knew it fell short. "It's cool. I like it." Was this my attempt at thanking him? What the hell was wrong with me?

"Look, I'll be back when I can. Since you don't have a phone, I guess, just don't go anywhere." He quickly added, "I don't mean to say, 'don't skip town' type of shit, but seriously, don't skip town while the investigation is still ongoing."

I wanted to tell him I wasn't an idiot and would obviously not be leaving the area, but instead I asked, "Do you know who he was?"

I figured maybe Wolf had been informed by now, and that made me think he probably knew everything about me, too. There was no chance someone hadn't pulled a background check on me down at the station. Not that I had anything criminal on my record, but I felt sure they would've been able to pull up something about my past—or maybe I had just seen too many movies? It's not like he was the FBI.

His face grew serious. "His name was Caleb Conners. Does that name sound familiar?"

"No," I said. And it didn't. It really didn't. I had never heard that name before, and I was still positive I had never seen him before, either. It must've been a completely random attack. I couldn't imagine being a planned target, because I didn't really know anyone here, and I hadn't made any enemies in my life as far as I knew.

These past few years, since Rocky had passed away, I'd been working hard to not have any real connections with people, and besides my moment of weakness which had brought me out to this state, specifically Indian Country, over a year ago, nobody knew me. So, the attack had to have been random, and damn it all to hell that I would be the lucky winner.

I guess a part of me knew it was lucky he hadn't chosen some other single woman's house—one who didn't have a Rosie to defend her and buy her time to act. He hadn't chosen someone whose dead loved one hadn't left them a loaded gun. Which reminded me…"Will I get Rocky's gun back?"

It was all I had left of his, besides a few shirts and sweatshirts. His mom, Leilani, and sister, Malia, had taken everything else. Malia would have grabbed the gun, too, had she'd known it existed.

Wolf's face looked grim. "Not for some time, if at all." Seeing my expression, he sighed. "Raven, it's registered in California under Rocky's name and is currently a piece of evidence."

I leaned up on my forearm, my hair further loosening from my hair tie. "I'm going to need that back, Wolf. It's all I have of Rocky's. It saved me as much as Rosie did."

Wolf hesitated before responding. "I'll see what I can do, but it's not going to be anytime soon, that's for certain. But I'll see."

I nodded. If that's the best he could do, and I was pretty sure it was, I had to be okay with it. "Alright. Thank you."

He smiled gently at me and turned from the doorway to leave.

"Wolf," I called for him—saying his name gave me a small thrill I didn't understand—and he turned. "Is this, like, okay to be happening? I mean, me being here at your home with you after…after what happened?" I was struggling to get the words out because I still couldn't believe what all had unfolded the night before.

He contemplated for a second and walked a few steps back into the room. "It's not illegal if that's what you're asking, but is it probably frowned upon?" He shrugged a little in answer. "It's fine, though. Seriously, don't worry about it. I'll handle any backlash if it comes out, which there shouldn't be. If there is, I promise, you won't be the one to deal with repercussions from this."

I heard what he was saying without saying it. That *I* couldn't get in trouble for being here, but *he* could potentially get in trouble. "Alright," I said, with a shaky breath.

His piercing eyes grew concerned. "Are you? You sure you're going to be fine here?"

"Positive." I forced a smile.

Once Wolf left, I lay in his bed for a while longer, lingering in the warm spot his body had made until it faded to only my own body warmth. My stomach eventually growled. I needed food and coffee—and soon. If I didn't, I was going to have one hell of a headache.

I wandered into Wolf's kitchen and turned on his Keurig. I poured water in the carafe and listened to the machine warming up. Light was streaming in through the windows off the kitchen and dining room, making the house bright. I searched for the coffee and all the man had were medium-roast generic-brand K-Cups. That would have to do.

His cup selection was bizarre and consisted of only five mugs, all Christmas-themed. In fact, all the crockery in his cupboards were the same Christmas theme as the mugs—a little green garland with red ribbon and the wording "Happy Holidays" in alternating green-and-red letters printed on them. Although it was getting close to the holiday season, I somehow doubted he was the type to be that festive, especially since there were no other holiday decorations out, let alone any décor at all. Not a plant or vase. Not a candy dish or tchotchke to be found.

I opened his fridge but didn't find any creamer; I could deal with milk, I supposed. The fridge was stocked with tons of fresh vegetables and fruits, the freezer full of different meat. His pantry was loaded with mostly whole foods like mixed nuts, pasta, and rice. Luckily, I found one small section of baking goods and grabbed the sugar. His spice selection was stacked with flavors I had never even heard of, and even more fresh vegetables and fruits were on his counter.

This guy is clearly a health nut.

I used a spoon to sprinkle some sugar into my coffee and stirred the milk in. I grabbed a banana—which I ate in three bites—and moved on to the berries in his fridge, then a handful of nuts. I felt a lot better after eating some of his health food stash.

Who was this guy, anyway? Was I being incredibly dumb going into a stranger's home only hours after a complete stranger broke into my own? What if he was just as bad as Caleb Conners? Or, what if he was a dirty cop? I'd seen *Training Day*.

I didn't really give clout to any of those questions as I thought them. I'd always been a good judge of character, always listening to my gut, and my gut hadn't raised any red flags when it came to Officer Rivers. Oddly enough, I figured he might just be a good guy. He sure seemed like one.

But still, something weird was going on at his place, regardless of just having moved in. It barely looked lived in. And what was with the Christmas-themed dishware? Also, he just conveniently had clean sheets on his bed? What bachelor had clean sheets on his bed? It was all strange.

I started to shiver; it was too chilly in his house. The thermostat on the wall in the living room showed it was only sixty-five degrees—way too low for my California soul. Unfortunately, the contraption looked too fancy for me to want to mess with it, so I went to his room and grabbed some sweatpants out of his dresser, putting them on over my Christmas pajama bottoms. I had to roll them up a few times so I wouldn't trip. I then found some of his socks and slid them on, seeing as how Officer Salone hadn't picked any out for me. Well, *picked* was not the right verb for what Salone had done. What she had done was more like grabbed whatever she'd seen when she opened my dresser drawers.

I retrieved the iPad from his dresser and bundled his dark-blue comforter around me as I sat cross-legged on his bed. After a few clicks, I had a delivery underway of sweatpants, a coat, jeans, a couple of plain long-sleeved shirts, t-shirts, sweaters, cute lacy underwear, socks, a bra for crying out loud, deodorant, toothpaste, a toothbrush, hairbrush, and hair ties. I wasn't sure when I planned to return to my house, but I didn't want to be sleeping there any time soon.

Despite it having been a year without any form of newer technology, using an iPad still came easy. I signed into my personal email to see if I had received any communication from one of the detectives I'd spoken with the night before. If Wolf knew who the assailant was, then I was sure I would need to speak to the detectives again.

Sure enough, an email from Detective O'Dell was at the top of my inbox. His message was short and sweet, letting me know they had more information and wanted to ask me more questions. He thoughtfully said he could meet me somewhere or I could come down to the station. I responded I would come to the station that evening. I really wasn't up for going back in the hot seat less than 24 hours later or going back to my house to get my car. Maybe they'd found out I'd lied to them, or maybe it was as simple as wanting to know if I knew Caleb, now that they'd identified him.

I was just about to push the iPad away when a ding sounded, and a notification window flashed on the screen. It was a notification for Messenger from someone named Lauren Hill. I went to swipe it away but accidentally clicked into it. I knew I shouldn't read it, but I couldn't help myself.

"Can you please make/bring the turkey and the green bean casserole dish Thursday? Drew is making his famous rolls I know you won't eat, and I'm making the stuffing that you also won't eat. Dad said he's making pies, a small ham, and Mom's mashed potatoes. I'm going to ask Jillian to make creamed corn and the tasty brussels

sprout dish with the bacon she made last year everyone loved. Oh, and maybe I'll have Sara and Devon put together some apps. What do you think?"

Of course, now it showed the message had been read. *Shit.* She was going to expect a response. As I was about to click out, response sounded. Wolf had responded! He must have seen it on his phone app. I really should've put the iPad down, but instead, I read his response.

"Yeah, sounds good. Of course I'm making the turkey! I will make the creamed corn, too, so tell Jillian not to bother."

Lauren's response came quickly after. *"Ok thanks!"* And then a moment later, *"I know it may be weird this year without Uncle Tommy's big crew and of course without Tiffany, but it'll still be good. I love you."*

Wolf's response was fast. *"Love you, too. I'll try to make it to Devon's game tomorrow night."* He capped it with a GIF of Shaq slamming a ball through the net.

A thumbs-up came from Lauren with a basketball emoji.

I clicked out of his Messenger and instantly felt guilty for reading what had obviously been a private conversation with his sister. I wondered if she was older or younger. Her profile picture had consisted of just a sunflower. I pushed away the urge to snoop through his Facebook, set the iPad back on his dresser, and then went back to his bed.

He had a family. A close one, from the sound of it, who spent holidays together and seemingly loved each other. I had never had that, at least, not that I could remember or that was real in any true sense. Just blurred memories of having it during the Good Years and a bit with Rocky. Even after Rocky died, I thought maybe I still had a place in his family, with his mom, sister, and the loads and loads of extended family members I had gotten to know and care for over the years. But for whatever reason, his mom had pushed me away, and that had been that.

I knew why; I couldn't act like I didn't. She blamed me. She blamed me for his death, and maybe she was right to. How could I not know he suffered from a heart condition? Had there been signs I should have seen?

No! *No.* I wasn't going there. I wasn't going to do that to myself again. I had done it enough.

I piled Wolf's pillows together, pulled the comforter over me, and leaned back. I needed to think about my current situation. Like the fact that I was lying in a police officer's bed who I'd met less than 24 hours earlier—eating his food, drinking his coffee, and wearing some of his clothes. I should have felt awkward and uncomfortable and gotten out as fast as I could. But he had comforted me in the night multiple times—granted, it'd been after he'd pointed a gun at me, but he hadn't shot me. He seemed unreal. There had to be something wrong with this dude, and I was willing to bet this Tiffany his sister mentioned was the key to that locked door.

I sighed. Now that I had eaten, warmed up, ordered what I needed, and decided Wolf was most likely a good guy, my mind went toward the night before, despite trying to avoid it.

I replayed every moment—well, every moment that was not a complete and utter haze—and with it, every emotion. But Rosie was alive, and that was ultimately what mattered. The second thing that mattered was that I didn't get convicted of any charges. The man probably had a family. Maybe one of them would press charges? Was it possible for the medical examiner or an investigator to know I had shot him purposefully in the crotch? Could an investigation really prove when I had turned the light on in relation to when I had fired the second shot? I shook my head as a knock came at Wolf's front door. My delivery.

Chapter Six

I spread my order out on Wolf's couch, ripping off the tags and stickers. Then threw all the clothes into Wolf's washing machine on a quick wash; I figured he wouldn't mind. I brushed my teeth with the new toothbrush and toothpaste. A small thing, brushing my teeth, but an action which made me feel a little better than the moment before when I'd been lost in my trepidation of the previous night's happenings.

While waiting for my clothes to finish in the wash, I decided to snoop around a little bit.

When I opened a door in the kitchen, expecting to see a utility closet, I found a staircase leading into the basement instead. Halfway down the stairs, I paused, considering maybe I was overstepping. However, I was intrigued, and my curiosity overcame his potential need for privacy.

The stairs led to a fully furnished basement with another bathroom and bedroom. The main space comprised of a large sectional couch, which had a pillow and blanket. Well, that explained why his bed upstairs had clean sheets; the man slept down here.

A massive TV and entertainment center was set up, and an indoor gym took up the entire right side of the main area. Opposite that was an office space with a medium-sized desk and a laptop. Several boxes, all labeled *Wolf's BOOKS*, were piled up next to an empty bookshelf. I didn't think any harm could come from organizing his books for him, so I opened the first box and got to work.

I loved to read. From a young age, I'd gobbled down book after book to escape the thoughts of losing my parents. My foster mom, Mama Elena, a tight-lipped old woman of Romanian heritage, never turned me down when I asked to go to the public library, which was nearly every other day.

Books kept me sane growing up and still continued to do so. Wolf had a massive collection of non-fiction, mainly covering psychology, criminal justice, and history, which I had not expected to see at all. In one of the boxes, I found two thin folded hard covers—diplomas. I opened one. It was from Marquette University. He had double-majored in psychology, and criminology and law studies. I opened the next, and it was a master's degree in psychology from the University of Wisconsin-Madison. *Well, damn!*

What in the hell was he doing being a regular cop? Maybe he wasn't a regular cop? This man was getting more and more interesting. Good looking, healthy, neat, and extremely educated. Although the non-fiction was quite intriguing, what amazed me even further was the boxes and boxes of fiction he had. They mainly included fantasy and science fiction. I smiled at the multiple copies of *The Hobbit* by J.R.R. Tolkien. He had six! All of them different editions and in mint condition, except for one. It was tattered and stained, along with multiple dog-eared pages. I opened the cover. A faded inscription read, "To my own little Bilbo, may you go on many unexpected adventures. Love, Mom." It was dated 1996.

Rocky had made me read *The Hobbit* and *The Lord of the Rings* books before watching each series. My smile faded into a frown. Even though it had been almost four years since Rocky, I still had moments that made my heart clench and eyes sting.

A beep sounding from upstairs signaled the washer was done. I put the last of Wolf's collection onto the bookshelf and headed back upstairs. Halfway up it hit me how lost I'd gotten in sorting Wolf's books and now the thought of being in a basement downstairs alone after what I had just been through felt terrifying. With that in mind, I skipped a step at a time and hauled up the stairs fast.

After transferring my clothes into the dryer, I decided to take a shower, knowing the clothes would be dry by the time I got out. Wolf only had a '2-in-one shampoo-conditioner for men, and even though I had washed my hair multiple times the night before, it did the trick as I scrubbed once again. With no bodywash to find, I realized he used bar soap. It seemed oddly intimate to use, but I did, and it probably should have grossed me out, but it didn't. It made me feel comforted. Or maybe that was just the smell. The soap smelled refreshing, the scent was woody but with a floral afternote. It was manly in the best way and I was instantly reminded of his arms around me and my head on his smooth muscular chest. *Ugh!* I needed to not think about that. I turned the shower water to ice-cold.

Once out of the shower, I brushed my hair with the newly delivered hairbrush and then braided it back into one simple plait. I paused to look at my reflection and took a deep breath. My face still seemed a little puffy from the night's cry session and from overall lack of sleep. It was only noticeable because I normally had defined cheeks, but now my cheeks seemed to smooth straight into my eyes. My usually bright green eyes looked dull, too, as if the irises themselves had cried out all their color.

I tightened the towel I had around me, opened the bathroom door to Wolf's room, and made my way down the hall to the dryer but stopped short and turned abruptly when I heard footsteps behind me. I couldn't help the jump and squeal that escaped my lips. I clutched the towel to my chest.

It was Wolf. "I'm sorry! It's just me. I'm back. I'd of called but…" he turned away setting his keys down on the counter in the kitchen. "I didn't realize you were in the shower…sorry."

"I'm just getting my clothes out of the dryer."

"Uh. Yeah. I'll just be in the kitchen." He said the words quickly and moved out of my view.

I wasn't sure why it felt so awkward with him seeing me in a towel. Since he'd seen *all* of me the night before. But it was. Somehow it *really* was. I grabbed the clothes out of the dryer as fast as I could without letting the towel fall and headed back to his room.

I quickly got dressed, relishing having soft, clean underwear of my choosing and a bra. After slipping on a dark blue long-sleeved cotton shirt, jeans, and socks, I headed out toward the sounds in the kitchen where Wolf was at.

"Um, thanks for letting me use your washer and dryer. I figured you wouldn't mind."

His back was to me, and he was frying chicken at the stove.

"Oh yeah, don't mind at all. I'm glad you felt comfortable enough to use them. Guessing that means it was alright being alone here?" he asked as he turned the pieces of chicken over with a pair of tongs. He had a kitchen towel slung over one shoulder; it looked so at odds with his police uniform.

"I guess. I mean it's daytime and all. Not to mention your home is very comfortable, even though it's in dire need of some decorating." I couldn't help myself.

He glanced back at me with a smirk. "You're not wrong. I just haven't found the time. Well, maybe it's more that I haven't made the time. But I'm glad you're comfortable here. It's nice to have…" Wolf looked back at the chicken, and cleared his throat. "It's nice to have someone to cook for," he finished.

It was odd. It was almost like he was about to say something completely different. Like maybe he too didn't want to be alone in his house, like maybe he thought it was nice to have me here?

"Are you hungry? This will be done soon."

I shook off my thoughts. How could I deny a home-cooked meal? I rarely cooked myself. "Uh, yeah. It smells amazing, thank you." I'd actually started to feel hungry again.

He had a plethora of spices out next to the sizzling pan, and the aroma filling the room made my mouth water. No one had cooked for me in a long time. Not that he was cooking for me, regardless of what he'd said the moment before, I knew it was for himself, and I was just an unplanned guest who needed to eat.

I walked over and sat on the one barstool at the counter and watched him work. "Do you usually come back home for lunch?" I was amazed at how fast he was now rinsing and chopping vegetables. His skills in the kitchen were clearly an indication that cooking for him was either a passion or had been a career at one point.

"No, not normally. Usually, I will pack a lunch and eat at the station or in the cruiser, depending. On my most motivated weeks I will meal prep for the entirety of the week. Were you able to find something you liked this morning?"

"I snagged some fruit and nuts. I will say though, you're definitely lacking in your coffee selection and creamer, but I managed."

For a split second he almost looked embarrassed but then smiled when he realized I was being facetious.

"Aw well, simple-black-coffee guy, here."

"I figured as much," I told him and watched as he expertly sliced a cucumber up. "Hey, I hope you know I really do appreciate everything you've done for me and I know it's weird I don't know anyone in the area after living here for a year, but I truly don't." I tried making eye contact with him so he could see the truth in my eyes, but he was focused on his preparations.

"So, why is that?" he asked nonchalantly as he moved the cooked chicken onto a cutting board and started slicing it into strips widthwise and then lengthwise.

I didn't want to answer that question but I'd opened the door for it I supposed.

"I specifically moved to Green Bay with the intent of keeping to myself, which is why I don't have any connections here. I didn't want any."

"Why Green Bay though? And why do you want to keep to yourself?" He divvied out the chicken onto two plates already brimming with different types of lettuces and chopped vegetables.

I really didn't want to get into all the nitty-gritty details of my life with this guy, especially considering he was a police officer. I'd keep it simple but honest with maybe a hint of diversion. "First of all, why not Green Bay? And, long story short: I've had a lot of loss in my life. More than most people my age. And after I lost Rocky, I decided to live a more solitary life. Look, I swear I'm not some crazy person who can't make friends, if that's what you were wondering."

You just didn't keep the ones you had for some reason, his face said, but instead, he politely answered, "I don't think you're a crazy person, and I'm sorry you've had to endure so much loss."

Coming from someone with a master's degree in psychology, I believed he felt that way. He didn't push further or ask anything else. I had anticipated a follow-up question or two, but he'd finished putting our salads together and was now taking out multiple toppings and dressings.

"I guess I should have asked if you have any food allergies?" A small look of concern crossed his face.

Who was this guy? Worrying about some random person's food allergies? Were people usually this thoughtful and I had just been such a loner lately I hadn't remembered?

I shook my head no. "I can eat anything and everything as far as I know. Oh, wow, this looks great!"

He slid a plate over to me and I loaded it with toppings—croutons, sunflower seeds, and cheeses—and chose a Caesar dressing. He then brought over two glasses of water and set one in front of me and made up his own salad.

Wolf was much simpler than me, and his toppings only consisted of some cheese, sprinkled salt and pepper, and a balsamic vinaigrette. He ate standing up across from the counter I was perched at, the plate easily balanced on his large hand.

For a while, we just quietly ate. It should have felt awkward, but it really didn't. I was sitting there with a cop I'd only just met, a man who'd seen me naked, a total stranger who'd comforted me and held me all night. But besides me knowing it should have been awkward, it wasn't, because something about his presence just calmed me.

"This is so good. Thank you," I said between bites. And it actually was. The chicken was perfectly seasoned and so flavorful. It was a restaurant-quality dish. "Where did you learn how to cook?"

He took a sip of his water and then set it down. "Glad you like it. Growing up, my parents made me and my sisters do 4-H, so that's how I learned to bake. Then I wanted to learn how to cook, so I started helping them with the dinner meals. My sisters are pretty good cooks, too."

I mentally winced, knowing I knew a little more about him than I should through my little snoop-session earlier. "So, sisters and no brothers?"

"Nope, no brothers, just two sisters; Lauren is three years older than me, and Jillian is two years younger. I also have a whole slew of cousins who are like brothers and sisters. What about you? Any siblings?"

Damn it, why did I ask him about himself? Of course, he was going to ask about me in return. And was he truly curious or just being a cop?

"No. Not really. I mean, I probably had a hundred or so foster brothers and sisters over the years, but no blood that I know of." I wanted to smack myself in the face for already telling him more about my past than I ever did with anyone nowadays. What was wrong with me?

I stood, grabbed my almost-licked-clean plate along with his empty plate he'd set on the island and brought them over to the sink.

He seemed a little caught off-guard by my forwardness in his kitchen. "You don't have to do that. I will get it later."

But that was not something I could let happen. I looked over my shoulder at him pointedly. "No chance. You cooked. I'll clean. The least I can do." I started rinsing the dishes and loading the dishwasher, hoping that was enough to steer the conversation away from me.

He turned his back toward the island and leaned against it, watching me rinse. "When did you go into foster care, if you don't mind me asking?"

Apparently, doing the dishes wasn't enough to change the subject. "I was six. My adoptive parents died in a car crash. I wasn't in the car."

That was always the follow-up question when I had to tell it: an exasperated noise, an apology, and then, *"were you in the car?!"* Like that somehow mattered, when I was living and breathing right there in front of them and my parents weren't. Wolf did have the decency to not make a sorrowful noise, but the apology was forthcoming.

"I'm so sorry."

I dried my hands on a towel and turned to him. The look he gave me was one of understanding and I didn't know why but it made me feel like crying. I held the tears in though.

"Yeah, it was a long time ago, and, like I said, I've experienced a lot of loss." I could see he was about to say something, maybe open up to me about his own losses he'd had to endure but I couldn't deal with that now. Surely the tears would fall if he did. So I changed the subject. "Can you take me to see Rosie now?"

He stood up straighter, taking the hint that I was done with that conversation. "Of course. I spoke to the vet this morning. They are expecting us."

And with that, I grabbed my coat and purse. I was going to see my girl!

Chapter Seven

Luckily, the drive to the veterinary hospital, BluePearl, was a quick ride, and we were there within a few minutes. After a brief conversation with the man at the front desk, Wolf and I were allowed to go straight back to see Rosie.

She had suffered a large head contusion from hitting the side of my dresser when that piece of shit threw her off him, and a side wound from the stabbing. She'd undergone surgery the night before to repair a punctured lung. The veterinarian explained, had she not been brought in when she was, the outcome would have been bleak. He was saying words to me like *hypoxia* and *pneumothorax* that I didn't understand, but I nodded anyway.

Rosie was currently sleeping from the anesthetic she had been given. She was a large, ninety-pound German shepherd-rottweiler mix. The mix meant her coloring looked more like a Rhodesian ridgeback with the reddish-brown fur than either of the breeds she was. In fact, she was mistaken for a ridgeback most of the time when we went for our walks.

The vet said he wanted to keep her a few days longer for proper rest, to keep her as immobile as possible, and to monitor for any infections, but after that, she'd be ready to come home.

My baby is going to be okay!

"You will need to ensure no running and jumping happens sooner than it should," he said, "and to give her medication to manage her pain. Try to keep any excitement for her to a minimum."

"Absolutely, I will. Thank you so much for everything." I was trying to hold myself together as best I could, but I could feel the dam about to break. "Can I have a moment with her?"

"Of course," the vet said, nodding.

He and Wolf walked a few feet away to give me some privacy with Rosie. I slowly stroked her snout. I couldn't stop the tears flowing and honestly didn't care if either man saw me crying. She had saved me, and she was *alive*. That bastard hadn't killed her. Even as I was crying, I was laughing on the inside. Sure, maybe it was some deep-seated evil part of me that thought this way, but it had served him right.

A memory from that night pounded into my brain—Caleb Conners, and his slew of cussing when Rosie had jumped on him. I wondered then if she had bitten him before he had stabbed her. Panic rose at the thought of her having any piece of him on her or in her. I turned a little abruptly toward the two men standing behind me and looked at the vet, "Can you make sure her teeth are brushed when she wakes up?"

He calmly walked over and stroked Rosie softly. "Absolutely, we will." I looked up at him appreciatively.

Wolf seemed to have picked up on my panic and came to my side. "Can I pet her?" he asked tentatively. I nodded as I wiped tears from my eyes and watched as Wolf slowly stroked Rosie's back, avoiding the bandaged areas. I leaned in and gave her small kisses on her snout. My sweet girl, my one true best friend.

What home could I even bring her back to?

With that thought in mind, we headed to the front so I could fill out paperwork and make a payment.

When we got back into Wolf's police cruiser and I didn't say anything, Wolf turned to me. "How are you holding up?"

I took a deep breath before responding, trying to ebb my fear. "I'm just thinking about how I'm going to have to bring Rosie back to the place she was injured. A place that was supposed to be safe." But Rosie had to have a home to come back to for her recovery.

Wolf nodded in understanding. "She looked good, though, don't you think? They are taking good care of her."

"Yes, she did. She's so strong." *Stronger than I'll ever be*, I didn't add.

A terrifying thought occurred to me. What if charges were pressed, if I was convicted of something and had to go away to prison—where would Rosie go? As scary as it was to be bringing her back home, at least she had a home with me to come back to. But what if that was off the table? Could I somehow get her to the reservation?

"Okay, so I'm obviously new to this, but...am I still not being charged with anything?" I tried to breathe normally, but my pulse had quickened.

He shook his head slightly. "No, you haven't been charged with anything. You would have been appointed a defense attorney if you didn't have your own and been in front of a judge already regarding a hearing; and if I felt like you were going to be charged with something, then I definitely would have taken you to a hotel last night and not my home." He said this with a slight lift to his voice, and I knew he was trying to make light of the very serious question I had asked.

He turned on the car and looked at me once more before backing out of the parking spot. After a moment on the road, he said, "The investigation is still ongoing and will be for, I imagine, a while longer. There's been a viral infection going around and it's taken a toll on our entire station. That's why I was working late last night. Salone and I don't usually work those hours, but we're down a few officers and helping out where we can. Unfortunately, the Investigative Unit has been hit really hard, and the medical examiner's report still hasn't come through. I'm sure it's pretty cut and dry, but those can take some time. Once the report comes through to our investigators, if there are any findings differing from what our forensic and crime analysts conclude...well, that could cause things to go even longer."

I sighed a little in relief. "Okay, well, I don't think I'm ready to stay at my house yet, and I guess with Rosie still being at the vet, there is time before I truly need to go back. Can you at least take me to my place so I can get some stuff really quick? Like my car, and my laptop, maybe some more clothes..." I trailed off thinking about entering my room—my room where a dead body had been.

"Yeah, of course. I have to head back to the station now, but how about when I get off work, I will pick you up, and we can swing by your place. With it being Monday tomorrow, I'm sure you have a job you need to be at?" He must not have watched the interviews I'd had with the detectives yet or he would have known that answer. Or, had he, and he was looking for holes in my story?

"I actually don't. I work from home for myself creating and selling printables." Wolf glanced at me with a questioning look. I couldn't help but smile. "So, like...invites to a baby shower, for example. I create those and then sell my product for people to print off themselves, or I can send them the product."

A look of understanding was now visible on his face. He gave me an appreciative look. "Oh, so you're an artist! That's cool."

I shrugged shyly. "I, um...I've never thought of myself in that way. But I guess some people would say a type of artist, yes. A creator of sorts. Luckily, my sales lately have been people wanting to print themselves, but I'm guessing I'll soon need my full office back with my printer and all my supplies in order to prepare shipments. But for now, if I can at least get my laptop, I can check emails and orders." Since I didn't have a phone, my laptop really was my only way to check emails and do my work. Plus, it was the only line of communication I had given to the detectives.

"I don't know how you do it, not having a phone." Wolf shook his head in disbelief. "No social media or anything?" Again, I found myself wondering if he was trying to get answers out of me in an investigative type of way. Technically, I did have social media—

personal accounts I hadn't been on since Rocky died and had never bothered to deactivate. There was no way he or O'Dell or whoever was on my case hadn't searched and found them.

"I do have social media accounts. I have some I use for my business, and I have personal ones, but I just don't get on them. Honestly, I probably can't even remember the passwords to even get back on them." Wait, that was a lie. My breath hitched a little. I knew the password. Rockysgirl4eva!. Corny as shit, but I had loved typing it in each time. A dull pain in my heart started, and I resisted the urge to rub my chest.

I changed the subject. "So, I hope I didn't overstep or anything, but I was sort of trying to keep myself busy this morning and kind of, sort of, unboxed all your books for you in the basement. Which, by the way, is a really cool spot. I stacked them in the shelves they were sitting next to."

His eyes widened a bit, the blue brighter than earlier. "Wow, really? No, I don't mind at all. I actually really appreciate it. I've been meaning to do that for a while now. I'll have to think of a way to repay you," he laughed, and I actually laughed, too. The sound was foreign to me. When was the last time I had laughed with someone?

I waved my hand passively. "It was fun. You have a really great collection and with the boxes labeled so clearly I couldn't help myself. I love books."

Wolf turned down his street. "Oh, yeah my ex had everything packed and labeled, ready for me to get the hell out."

Ah-ha! Cheater, cheater, pumpkin-eater, I almost shouted. I knew there had to be something with this guy. He had to have cheated on his wife, I mean why else would any woman rid themselves of him? He couldn't be that hot, that incredibly kind to some random woman, and not have something wrong with him.

I felt relieved. This guy had been seeming too good to be true, and now I could push any pathetic fantasies of some big, sexy cop saving the day out of my head. Not that any of those fantasies had creeped in, but he was gorgeous, and he had made me feel so comfortable, safe even. The thought of him being a cheater reassured my brain I could not and would not develop real feelings for him. Not that I ever would, anyway. But once a cheater, always a cheater, Mama Elena had drilled into my head.

I hoped my smug relief wasn't showing on my face. "Well, I don't mind unpacking more stuff. If the other boxes are labeled like the ones I saw, I'll open the ones that I think I can easily find a place for or put away."

Wolf pulled into his driveway and put the car in park. He turned to me, his eyes sparkling bright. "Yeah? I mean, my sisters haven't even offered to do that. I'll take you up on it. And seriously, I'm going to think of the perfect way to repay you."

Despite him likely being a cheater, I couldn't help the warm blush slip cross my cheeks. "It's the least I can do while you let me stay with you." I quickly realized I had made a mistake. I was assuming he was going to keep letting me stay with him. Which was ridiculous. Once I had my car and some belongings, I could really just go to a hotel and be pretty comfortable and self-sufficient. Well, I'd be physically comfortable, but not mentally. I looked out the front windshield and stared at his closed garage door.

I clasped my hands in my lap. "I didn't mean to assume I could stay another night. I will go to a hotel once I get my car and things tonight, but I'm sure I can get a few boxes unpacked until then."

Wolf tapped his thumb on the steering wheel a few times. "Is that what you want? Because you really aren't putting me out, and…" I dared to look at him when he paused, and his blue gaze captivated me. I couldn't look away. "I don't want you to feel alone."

I winced a little at the reality of his words, breaking the spell between us. He cleared his throat. "I just mean, if you're not ready to be alone yet, especially without Rosie, you can stay with me longer."

I was quiet for a while, even though I knew what I wanted to do immediately.

"Yes, I would like to stay with you."

Feeling so much relief at being able to stay with him was annoying. Had I let myself become so deprived of human friends and real, quality interactions, the thought of not staying with this random cop at his home almost made me panic? Or was it simply he'd been there for me and comforted me at my most vulnerable after a traumatic event? Was I associating him with safety? Or, fuck, maybe it's simply he's hot as hell and I hadn't been laid in months. Who was I kidding? It'd been at least two years.

"Great, and maybe seeing your progress will motivate me to finally start unpacking some stuff," he said.

It was odd to me, how casual and friendly he acted after having held me all night, comforting me.

I smiled back. "If there's even anything left for you to unpack. I'm very efficient."

Chapter Eight

I was, indeed, quite efficient. After Wolf left for the station, I'd gone back down to his basement to see what other boxes I could unpack. I'd found a few labeled with his name and "décor". They were full of lamps, pillows, framed pictures, and paintings. In the one spare bedroom in the basement, I found side tables and a rolled-up rug. I went about moving things upstairs. I unrolled the cream-colored rug with a gray interwoven design and placed it in front of the couch. Then I arranged the side tables on either side of his couch. The lamps were next and then a few throw pillows.

One of the paintings I unboxed was a beautiful lake scene with grays, greens, and blues and it went perfectly with his couch and the green pillows I had found. I located a few hooks and hung the painting above his couch. The final touch was a soft, gray crocheted throw blanket.

I rested a small framed picture of Wolf and a man whom I assumed was his dad; they had the same nose and eye shape and matching smiles, but where Wolf had blond hair, the man's was dark-brown with white sprinkled throughout. In the picture, they stood in front of a house on a lake. His dad stood a couple of inches shorter than him with his arm over his son's shoulders. The other picture I set up was of Wolf in front of a birthday cake holding up a shirt that read *Best Uncle Ever*. His smile was infectious, and I found myself smiling back at it.

Some of the pictures I came across had women in them and I wasn't sure if one might have been his ex, so I left those frames in a box for him to go through. I managed to hoof a coffee table up the stairs and placed it on the rug. I had also seen an unused entertainment table down there, and although I really couldn't stand his TV on the ground, I wasn't strong enough and my limbs weren't long enough to bring it up the stairs on my own. Unfortunately, it would have to wait. I pondered for a minute why Wolf had movers bring all this stuff down to the basement bedroom, but figured it really was none of my business. My only guess was he'd planned on having roommates.

Feeling unbearably tired all of a sudden, I lay on the couch, and, before I knew it, I was out. I must have been beyond exhausted because when I woke up in a cold sweat, rolling my body up quickly, I noticed the throw blanket had been draped over me, and I could hear sounds coming from the kitchen.

"Wolf?" I said hesitantly, a little panicked.

He swiftly came around the corner, holding a glass of water, still in his cop garb. "Sorry. Did I wake you?"

"It's fine. I didn't even realize I passed out." I rubbed the back of my neck.

Wolf waved a hand across the room. "The place looks great! You weren't kidding, you definitely are efficient."

I watched him look around appreciatively.

"I didn't realize I had some of this stuff. I hadn't really taken inventory of what Tiffany had been willing to part with." His head tilted as he assessed my glistening face. "Did you sleep okay?" By the concerned look in his eye, I knew he was referring to night terrors.

I wiped my forehead with the back of my hand. "Yeah…I think so. I wasn't able to lift the table up for the TV. It really shouldn't be on the ground like that."

He laughed softly. "Thanks for trying. I can get it later. You need a minute? Or are you ready to go stop by your place?" He took a drink of water.

I got up off the couch. No, I wasn't really ready to go back inside my home, not at all, but life had to go on just as it always did when trauma occurred in my life.

"Not really, but let's go anyway," I said. "I need my stuff."

"If you tell me what you want and where it is, I can grab it for you. You don't have to step foot in there if you're not ready yet."

I appreciated the offer. More than he would ever know but I had to deny it. "No. I'll have to live there again sooner or later, right? It's my home. I'll be fine. I just need to get it over with."

The drive from Wolf's place to my own, in the Aspen Arches neighborhood, was only about a seven-minute drive. Which was somehow wild to me—knowing this man had been so close to me this whole time. When we pulled up, I looked around. There she was; home sweet home. The gray-brown exterior looked daunting and gloomy. My home lacked curb appeal, but previously, driving into my neighborhood had always brought me joy. At that moment, though, I felt the opposite. I felt darkness. I wondered then how the police had known to come.

"Did one of my neighbors call 911?"

"There were multiple calls coming in for gunfire and screaming," Wolf said as he parked his truck.

I hadn't even made a point to really get to know my neighbors. Part of me felt guilty about that now. It was a seemingly safe neighborhood, and I bet they were all decent people.

"Do you guys have any leads on why he targeted me? My house?"

Wolf cleared his throat. "At this point, it's being considered a random attack—a crime of opportunity. Surveillance footage was pulled from the grocery store you were at earlier, and he is seen following you out of the store. His DNA is being run to see if we can connect him with some other similar attacks in the area."

Other similar attacks? Other women had gone through what I had, but likely worse. Other women had smelled that foul creature in their homes. The non-existent smell still an affront to my senses.

Wolf reached out and his fingers grazed me lightly on my forearm. "Raven, I am really sorry it had to happen to you." His apology, like the others before, was genuine, and I did appreciate it. Even though I couldn't bring myself to respond properly to him. I mumbled a thank-you.

My home was a small two-bedroom, one-bath house with a detached small garage and pretty decent-sized fenced backyard, which had been a huge selling point since I had Rosie.

Once we were inside, I instinctively breathed through my mouth instead of my nose. I knew my room had been cleaned, but I did not want to smell it. Him. The wretched stench from last night.

I moved quickly and methodically, feeling spooked everywhere I turned.

I moved past the dining table and looked into my kitchen, noticing the large cast iron skillet with leftover oil still sitting on my stove, the cutting board and knife still sitting out. I had actually cooked the previous evening, a rare event, but hadn't gotten to cleaning the handwash items, planning to get to them in the morning. It would have to wait. Besides that small mess, my home was clean and tidy. I tried not to dwell on Rosie's empty bed next to her kennel in the living room. She'd be home soon, and hopefully all would go back to normal. I doubted it, even as I thought it.

I went into the spare room I had converted into my office, which was off my kitchen, and grabbed my laptop, charger, and computer mouse, and shoved it all into the laptop bag. Then I grabbed my car keys from my kitchen counter and my favorite knitted purple beanie, slipping it on. That was all. Nothing more mattered, and I could do without for a few days. I was *not* going into my bedroom—couldn't stomach it.

My breathing had picked up the moment I had walked in, and now it felt like I had just sprinted up a hill. I didn't want to be in here any longer. It was as if the walls were starting to close in on me, and the sounds of floorboards creaking under my steps and Wolf's were wreaking havoc in my brain. I had to get out of there. Preferably before I had a full-blown panic attack, which I had never experienced, but I was starting to understand the gist.

I headed toward the front door. "Okay, done. I'm ready to go."

Wolf quickly followed up behind me. "You sure you don't want to grab anything else?"

I walked out the door and threw back over my shoulder, "Nope, I'm good. I forgot I have to meet with Detective O'Dell. He said he has more questions for me."

"Do you want me to go with you? I can work on a report while you're with O'Dell."

It was a nice offer but I heard the hesitancy in his voice. He was just being thoughtful, because we both knew it would surely raise questions from his peers about why he was with me.

"No, I appreciate it, but I will be fine. Hopefully it goes quickly and I'll head back over to your place after."

I locked my front door and Wolf walked me to my car before heading to his truck. He waited patiently for me to drive off before he did so himself. I'd been needing something to focus on, and driving was helpful. It gave me something to take my mind off of being in my home where a rapist-killer-psycho had been. Where someone had died. Where I had *killed* someone. Where Rosie had been injured.

But as I drove closer to the station, I was certain this was it for me. Certain O'Dell was going to charge me with whatever charge shooting someone purposefully in the crotch was, and I'd be arrested. The next time I saw Wolf would probably be from behind bars with his beautiful blue eyes looking at me with disgust. Not that it mattered what he thought.

Thankfully, my time with Detective O'Dell was completely uneventful and did not include him reading me my rights or putting me in handcuffs. The very serious man just wanted to know if the name Caleb Conners meant anything to me and if there were any other details I could remember from the day of the attack or even the days leading up to it. I tried my best to recount everything I had done that day again, but nothing new had come to mind beyond what I had said the night before.

"That's all I need from you today. Stay diligent in checking your email for communication from us. And it goes both ways, Ms. Lowe. Contact me if you recall anything else which might deem helpful to this investigation. Even the smallest detail."

"I will, Detective."

I left the station, still replaying all the happenings of my days prior to the attack the entire drive to Wolf's.

"How'd it go?" Wolf asked, as soon as he opened his front door.

"Fruitless. Nothing new except questioning if the name, Caleb Conners was familiar." I set my purse down on the newly placed end table and took a seat on the couch and stared off, again questioning myself regarding the name.

"Do you want to talk about it?"

The free therapy session with this more than qualified individual was enticing, however, I wasn't even sure where to begin, nor had the energy.

I shook my head, trying to shake the thought of myself in some office, laying on a couch, Wolf with a notepad asking me about my feelings. "No. Thank you though. You're really sweet for caring." I gave him a small smile. It's all I could muster.

He didn't press, thankfully, and clicked on the Sunday Night Football game. He must have showered when I was gone, because he'd changed into dark-gray joggers, a long-sleeved black Green Bay Packers shirt and his hair was a little damp.

Everyone in Wisconsin was a Packers fan. I'd learned that as soon as I'd arrived and quickly bought some gear. Not because I wanted to fit in, but because I didn't want to stand out.

"Anything in particular sound good for dinner?" Wolf asked. He walked into the kitchen and opened the fridge, peering in. I sat up straighter, realizing my stomach needed nourishment.

"Oh, you don't have to make me anything. In fact, I can order us food. Do you have any favorite spots for take-out?" It dawned on me I should have picked up some food on my way back to his house. The man was letting me stay with him, the least I could do was unbox some stuff for him and feed him!

He looked out from behind the fridge door. "I cook most nights, and I enjoy it. I'm going to cook dinner for you, Raven. So, what do you want?"

He actually enjoyed cooking? Well, if his salads were amazing, I couldn't wait to try what else he could make. "Truly, I'm not picky when it comes to food. Whatever you cook, I'll eat." And that was the truth. I loved most foods, and even foods I wasn't exactly fond of, like sweet pickles, I still ate if served them.

"How about pulled pork tacos?" He started to grab spices out of the pantry.

My mouth watered at the thought. "Sounds good to me. I'll come help you." I moved to stand but his answer stopped me.

"No, I'm good. I'm kind of a kitchen snob. I'll let you know when it's done. Just relax and watch the game."

Shit, he's too good to be true. I hated cooking, mostly because I just wasn't very good at it. Growing up, Mama Elena had been a fantastic cook but never wanted me in the kitchen. I'd usually tend to the foster babies in the home while she cooked our meals.

While Wolf cooked, I continued to sit on the couch staring at the TV. But I didn't see the game. I didn't hear the sounds of the whistles or the clash of football gear. Instead, I heard creaking floorboards and Rosie growling. I heard Caleb's voice calling me a fucking bitch. I heard gunfire. I didn't feel the couch underneath me, either. I felt tangled sheets and cold metal in my hands. I didn't smell the surely delicious food being cooked in the kitchen. I smelled the tangy scent of blood and something worse; urine and stale shit and gun smoke.

I killed someone.

Yes, someone who'd planned to hurt me, someone who'd hurt my baby girl, but I'd killed him. He had thoughts and feelings and probably a family, and now he was gone. God, did he have children? Did I take a father away from his kids? But even so, maybe I'd given those children a gift?

He had been a despicable human being; I'd discovered that in just the few words we'd exchanged. If I knew anything, I knew I didn't regret it. I regretted how I was feeling now. I regretted having posttraumatic stress and how scared I was to be in my own home. I regretted a lot of things, but I did not regret killing him. I even wanted to regret he'd chosen my house, but I couldn't, because he hadn't hurt anyone else and would never again, thanks to me and thanks to Rosie. What did that say about me? Was I a bad person? Would people now consider me a murderer? But what I'd done hadn't been murder. No, no, it had been self-defense. The first and the third shot anyway. The second shot, well, it had been something else. But I didn't regret that, either. A part of me even regretted lying and leaving out the details of it when I'd given my statement. I didn't know how investigations worked but I was guessing all my neighbors were being questioned and their home surveillance taken. What would they say about the gunshots and the timing between them? Was there some way to tell the gun had only been fired once before I turned on my light instead of twice? Was there some way for them to know that?

Panic started rising in me. What would Wolf think of me when he found out I was a liar? Not that I gave a shit what the guy thought. It didn't matter if he thought I was a liar or not. We weren't friends, we barely knew each other. Still, the thought of him finding me a liar was eating at me.

I needed to stop thinking about what had happened. I shook my head and forced myself to blink quickly to bring myself back to the present moment. Gradually, the sounds of the game and tasty smells permeating from the kitchen worked their way into my senses. The soft fabric of Wolf's couch under my hands kept me grounded.

"Dinner's ready," Wolf announced, and I took a deep breath before standing and walked over to the kitchen table. "Is it a good game?"

Caught off guard by the question, I went with honesty. "To tell you the truth, I was a little zoned out, but it looks like Tampa Bay is up by three."

Wolf looked at me knowingly. "Yeah, I'm sure you have a lot on your mind. I know you said you didn't want to talk about it but if you change your mind and want to talk about what happened—in a non-investigation-type way—I'm here for you," he said carefully and then touched my arm softly.

I ignored the spark of pleasure that shot through me at his touch and instead of answering I pursed my lips and smiled with my eyes at him.

He got the hint and chuckled. "Or…I could just grab you a beer."

I sighed with relief. "Now you're talking! Obviously, I don't condone using alcohol as a means to not deal with ones own feelings, but yes I would love one, thank you."

"Of course," he laughed, "dig in, and I'll get it."

My appetite had completely vanished due to the deep despondency that had rolled in, but now the sights and smells were so fantastic I slowly savored my first taco.

As I ate, I watched him in the kitchen. He sliced up a lime, opened two beer bottles, and wiped clean the neck and the rim with a paper towel. Then he swiped the rim and neck quickly with the lime slice before squeezing the rest of it into the beer and pushing it down into the bottle. After that, he picked up the saltshaker and shook salt where the lime juice was on the beer bottle. He brought the beers over and sat across from me at the table, handing me one as he tipped his own toward me. "To…my Friday, I guess."

We clinked our bottles together, and I felt a little silly for doing so. I knew he was trying to make things seem normal, but nothing about this situation was normal. I wasn't supposed to be here; I knew that. And I knew he could get in trouble for this. He really didn't seem to care, though. If this entire incident had revealed anything to me, it was that I was lonely. I was a self-inflicted loner, for sure, but some small part of me wasn't able to fight off the feeling of being a loser for not having any connections in Wisconsin. I couldn't help the co-worker and family part… well, not entirely true, either, but I could have made friends or at least been friendly with my neighbors by this point. I'd had multiple opportunities with people out and about who'd approached me and struck up conversations. People in the Midwest were very friendly; even, apparently, the police.

I took a sip, and the bite of salt and lime was a perfect addition to the Mexican beer and tacos.

When was the last time I clinked glasses with a friend? I didn't even remember. Such a common, fun gesture, but I had no memory of ever doing it. I'd been perfectly fine—and to some extent, happy—in my loner bubble until this Conners piece of shit had to ruin everything. Now more than ever, it was obvious I needed human interaction and maybe even a few friends. But would I allow myself that?

We made small talk about the food and my work while we ate and drank our beers. I tried to keep my personal details to a minimum.

When my beer was gone, Wolf asked, "Can I get you another?"

"I do want one, but I'll get it. Do you want one, too?"

"Sure. Thanks. Want a couple more tacos?"

"Yes, please!" I answered eagerly, and he got up to fix our plates with a smile on his face. I had already eaten three, but they were just so good, and in my defense, they were street-taco-sized. The homemade lime-cilantro sauce he'd drizzled on them was downright addicting. I could definitely enjoy a couple more—or just drink the sauce on its own, for that matter.

I opened the fridge to grab the beers and stopped short, noticing three different types of new coffee creamers sitting on the top shelf. He must have bought them on his way home from work. I bit my lip to keep from smiling and grabbed two beers. I prepared them just as I had seen him do, and I could feel his eyes on me. To assess if I was doing it right, maybe? Or was he watching me for other reasons?

The sounds of him assembling the tacos resumed. "So, you said you majored in art, but you seemed hesitant to call yourself an artist."

I laughed. "Okay, so yes, I majored in Digital Arts from USC…umm, that's University of Southern California."

"I know USC. Clay Matthews played there before getting drafted to play for the Packers. A great school."

"Oh, right. He did!"

We sat back down as we continued our conversation, and he handed me my plate with two tacos as I slid him his beer. "Anyway, yes, I am an artist," I continued. "But don't get excited. I can't paint anything to save my life. I can't sculpt. But on the computer, I can create." He nodded, not looking entirely convinced, and I laughed a little. "I have so much appreciation for the arts—artists in general. I just want to be clear regarding my scope of abilities."

"Okay, well, I guess I see what you're saying, but you *are* an artist, and that's really cool," he said, as if I was special somehow.

"You haven't even seen my work! Maybe you'll disagree after you see it." I winked at him and took a swig of my beer. *I actually winked at him. What the hell?* The beer was already going to my head. "What about you?" I asked.

"What about me?" he said, looking at me.

His eyes were truly dazzling. The light overhead made the blue sparkle. It was hard not to get lost in them but I forced the next sentence out of my mouth. "I saw your diplomas down there. You, sir, are quite the learned fella." *Learned fella? What?* Oh, yes, I was definitely feeling good.

He chuckled shyly and took a sip of his own beer before answering. "I really enjoy learning and reading, as you could probably tell. I don't like not knowing things—it bothers me in a sense. I knew at a pretty young age I wanted to get into police and investigative work, I wanted to help people, and in order to do that, I knew I needed to understand people's thought processes. That's where the double major in psychology and criminology came into play. Then after undergrad, I decided I wanted to roll right into my master's because I found it all really fascinating. I figured the better I understood the human psyche, the better I could solve cases."

But he wasn't a detective, he was just a regular patrol cop, wasn't he?

"Plus…" he said, taking another sip of his beer.

I couldn't help but look at his mouth on that beer bottle. His lips were perfectly full, and his mouth curved in a naturally sexy way. I just couldn't help but think of it around my—

"…you get paid way better in the department when you have a degree."

I mentally smacked myself in the face for my mind trailing. I looked down at my own beer and took another drink before responding. "Oh really? I didn't know that. So how long have you been a police officer?"

Something in his expression changed for a split second before he responded. "I've been with the department for going on twelve years now. Joined right after I finished up my master's program when I was twenty-three."

Twelve years, which would make him thirty-five-ish, exactly what I had been thinking. "How long were you married, if you don't mind me asking?"

He stood up. "No, I don't mind." He grabbed our plates, and we moved into the kitchen together to start cleaning. "I met Tiffany my junior year of undergrad and we started dating pretty quickly. We broke up a few times here and there in the early years but ultimately got married after I joined the department."

"So, you were married for a long time. No kids?"

He looked over at me. "No. No kids. She never wanted any."

He was probably wondering why I was asking him these questions. I was wondering the same thing, but I couldn't stop myself. For some reason, I wanted to know what had happened with this guy for him to have everything great in life and fuck it up with cheating. Poor Tiffany was probably crushed.

"What about you? Any kids?"

That threw me off, and I whipped my head toward him, feeling some of my hair coming out of my braid. I composed myself quickly, "Why, Officer Rivers, you and I both know you've probably done a background and/or Googled me. I think you know the answer is no."

He did have the decency to shrug a little abashedly. "Well, you aren't wrong, but there wasn't a whole lot out there on you—which is a good sign—so anything is possible."

"A good sign I'm not some evil temptress murderer like I'm sure Officer Salone thinks I am," I said as I loaded the dishwasher.

He got serious then. "No. She doesn't think you're that. She's just been in our line of work a long time, and after you've seen and heard basically nightmares coming to life, you just lose a little faith in humanity is all. I think Salone has reached that point in her career." He wiped the kitchen table off with a towel.

"Hmm. Well, wouldn't you say maybe it's time for her to retire?" I asked.

"I would, actually, yes. But she hasn't mentioned retirement to me once, and she is a very good officer. One of the best, even if she can be quite jaded at times. She's had my back more times than I can count." He walked back into the kitchen, close to me. He folded the towel he'd been using and set it next to the sink.

How he'd spoken of the gruff older woman left me a little in awe, because he'd spoken as if he was proud of her; the camaraderie between the two rang clear.

After cleaning up, we watched the end of the game together, sitting side by side on the couch—me, snuggled up with the throw blanket.

Wolf knew a lot about football, spouting off details about the two teams as if he was a fan of theirs. But then started talking about the Packers, and it was clear he was a Packers fan through and through. I chimed in here and there with what little I knew about the actual statistics. I liked watching football, even understood the game, and knew the names of most of the players on the Packers and big-time players on other teams. Remembering stats or plays from seasons past, I usually couldn't care less about, and yet I found myself intrigued by the amount of knowledge and memory this man had regarding the sport. We each had two more beers by the time the game was over.

I stood and stretched my arms above my head and felt the cool air brush against the sliver of exposed skin from where my top had lifted. I noticed Wolf's eyes on me, but he realized I'd caught him looking and quickly busied himself with turning off the TV. I wondered if I saw a blush.

"Ready to crash?" he asked as he stood, reaching for the empty beer bottle in my hand. I handed it to him, and our fingers brushed softly against each other. It was my turn to blush.

"Yeah," I said, but I wasn't exactly. I was tired, but I wasn't ready for my mind to race again like it had before dinner. I knew the moment I lay down, I was going to think about what happened, about Rosie alone at the veterinarian hospital, and our home now soiled by Caleb Conners. I just wanted to forget it all happened.

Wolf took our empty bottles into the kitchen, and I watched him as he checked that the doors were locked and turned his front porch light on. He clicked off the inside lights except for one side lamp, and then we both headed down the dark hallway into his room and he flipped on the bedroom light.

I stopped a few feet into his room, staring at the bed. I started to hear the floorboards creaking and growling in my head. Wolf stepped in and stopped behind me.

"Raven? What's wrong?"

I didn't want to do it again. I didn't want to feel sad or shocked or angry or all the things I had been feeling. But going back into my home earlier had brought most of those feelings back to the surface.

"Nothing. I'm fine." I shook my head, still looking at the bed.

I didn't think he was convinced. However, he left it alone. "Alright. I'm going to grab another blanket for the bed." He turned, but before he could make it a full step, I grabbed his hand. It was so big compared to mine. He quickly turned back to me, looking down at where I grasped him, and then up to my face.

I looked up at him. He was at least a foot taller than me. "I don't want to do what we did last night. I don't want you to hold me while I cry."

His face became grave. "I'm sorry if I overstepped. Or if I made you feel uncomfortable. I just—"

"No!" I quickly said. "You were great. You've been great. That's not what I mean. I mean tonight, I just want to forget. I don't want to cry and feel sorry for myself."

His face smoothed into understanding, and his breath hitched as he took a step toward me, the hand I had grabbed now holding mine softly.

"Tonight…I want to forget about what happened. Do you think you can help me forget, Wolf?"

I had never been a shy person by any means, but at that moment, I was being very bold. Bolder than I had been in a long time. Maybe the four beers had something to do with it? I was opening myself up for rejection, but could I really handle that?

He took a step toward me, and I moved a step back instinctively against his wall, bumping his light switch off. We were dark silhouettes in the room, and Wolf's free hand came up to cup the side of my face and I looked up at him, his thumb smoothing against my jaw and my bottom lip. "I can help you with that." Then his mouth found mine. His lips were so soft and smooth. The first kiss was tentative and sweet; his tongue swept into my mouth as I moved mine against his in the perfect dance. I dropped his hand and moved both of mine to his chest. God, he was so fit. The feel of his muscled chest under my fingertips made my heart beat faster, and I could feel his own heart speeding up as well.

He moved his now free hand to my backside and grabbed. Not too hard but not soft at all. It was a grab that made me wonder if he'd wanted to do that from the moment he saw me, saw me standing there naked. He pulled back from our kissing and, his voice sounding huskier than I'd heard before, said, "God, I bet you get so fucking wet."

Hello! I had not expected that. He moved to kiss my neck, and I was thankful it was dark so he couldn't see my eyes popping out of my head. Oh yes, this guy had definitely cheated on his wife. Who talked like that in the bedroom? I mean, I wasn't hating it, but it was clear he knew exactly what he was doing. In fact, those words had the exact effect he'd wanted them to have; I instantly felt warm and slick between my legs.

We both moved to take off each other's shirts at the same time and then stopped, deciding to remove our own. Once our shirts were off, his hand reached around my back and flicked my bra off as he kissed me again. Way too practiced—it came off on his first try, and I let it slide off my arms and hit the ground. His hands instantly went to my breasts, and I arched a little and leaned my head back. His mouth went to my neck again and he moved his hands down my sides and cupped my ass, lifting me off the floor as my arms came around his neck. His face was perfectly centered with my chest, and he lightly nipped at the sides of my breasts and moved me to the bed.

He laid me down and stood, taking his pants off. From the faint light streaming in through the crack in the door, his naked silhouette looked like a Greek god…or maybe more like a sex god. He was incredible, and he was ready—very ready.

I instantly realized this was exactly what I needed. I slipped my pants and underwear down, and he grabbed them, pulling them off and flinging them to the floor. I squirmed back toward the pillows, and he was easing down on top of me before I knew it. His mouth moved up my stomach and to my chest. The feeling of his lips and tongue licking and sucking my nipples was pure bliss. I let a small moan out, and one of his hands left my side and slowly moved to caress my inner thighs. One and then the other.

He moved his hand toward my middle and found out just what he'd betted on. "I knew it." His voice was so sexy. "So fucking wet. I want to taste you."

But I didn't want that. I mean, I did. Of course, I did. So badly. But that had always seemed so much more intimate to me than sex, and I didn't want this to get too intimate. I just wanted to forget, and he was doing such a good job of helping me achieve that.

As he lowered his body farther down the bed, he trailed kisses, soft and sweet, down my torso. Farther and farther down. I grabbed his shoulders and lightly tugged him up. He got the hint because his kisses started to trail back up and instead, his fingers found his mouth's intended target. My breath caught.

He slowly moved two fingers in and out, picking up speed but not too fast. His thumb moved to my most sensitive spot, and he stopped kissing me. "How badly do you want to forget?"

I couldn't believe this guy was talking to me like this. Rocky had never talked during sex. Made plenty of moans and groans but never talked dirty. The other couple of guys I had hooked up with since Rocky also hadn't been talkers. This was new. It was different. It was fucking hot. I couldn't talk like that. I would sound like an idiot, probably call him Daddy or something and ruin the mood. But I had to answer him, so I said, "Badly. Please, make me forget everything."

He grumbled sexily and pulled his fingers out of me. He started to move up, and I placed my hand on his chest stopping him before he inserted himself into my ready and eagerly waiting center.

"A condom?" I asked quietly.

"Oh, shit. I'm sorry. Yeah, obviously."

He reached over easily and pulled the drawer to his nightstand open and grabbed a strip of condoms out. He had the condom out and on in less than five seconds. I tried not to let the *cheater, cheater, pumpkin-eater* thoughts ruin the mood.

Straddling me, he moved his hands down my body on either side. He grabbed my breasts and leaned down. Sucking one and then the other. All cheater thoughts disappeared from my head. He moved then and lowered his face to mine as we found each other's lips again. My hands, feeling him—his arms, his back, his ass. He was so smooth and perfect. He started to press into me slowly.

"Do you think you'll…um…fit?" I asked softly.

He smiled against my mouth. "Let's find out." Then with one quick thrust, he slammed into me. Jolts of pleasure shot throughout my body, and I unleashed myself. Gripping on to his back and wrapping my legs around him, I screamed a little. But he didn't respond to my scream. He just performed. As if my ask to forget was his mission and he planned to execute it to a T. He lifted me up from the bed, his hand moving to my backside while I kept my arms around his neck. We moved apart and together over and over. The friction from him pressed against me, setting me off while he slammed into my g-spot again and again and again. Sparks of gratification ricocheted throughout me. I couldn't control my screams of pleasure as I bit down on his shoulder. He must have liked that because he groaned in satisfaction and came in shuddering spasms, holding me tightly against him.

He slowly eased us back down onto the bed and kissed my now-swollen lips. I threaded my fingers through his hair, and I kissed him back. He was still inside me, but I didn't want to stop kissing him. He finally pulled away, gave me a final kiss, pulled out and lifted off me, and went into his bathroom.

I lay there feeling…feeling fucking *great*.

After a moment, he returned from the bathroom. I switched places with him and shut the bathroom door. Naked, I looked at myself in the mirror. My face was full of color; there was a light red coming through my cheeks, and my lips were plump. A little rush of excitement went through me. For what exactly, I didn't know. I didn't really care.

He had done what I'd wanted.

Chapter Nine

I stared into the darkness, wrapped in Wolf's arms. He was warm and smooth and comfortable. I couldn't help but enjoy it. This couldn't happen again, I knew. I couldn't let myself get attached or entrenched in these feelings, but the point had been to forget about everything that had happened—and not just from the attack, but from all of it. My whole damned, sad life. He had done that for me, and I greedily wanted it to last even for just a little bit longer. Naked but warm in his arms, I quickly fell into a blissful sleep.

When I woke in the morning, I was still curled up in Wolf's arms. I was pleased to find no drool had come out of my mouth nor were my eyes crusted with dried tears. So that was an improvement. I also hadn't recalled waking in the middle of the night with a nightmare; another plus. I slowly slipped out of his arms to the edge of the bed.

"Come back," he mumbled, his voice gruff and sexy.

I wanted to reach out and caress his beautiful, sleepy face, and that—that was not okay. That was not how this was going to go.

"I'm going to take a shower," I whispered. I left the warmth of the bed, his arms tiredly outstretched for me as he continued to sleep.

As I took my shower, I tried not to replay the night's activities and instead focused on how it was never going to happen again. I tried to figure out how the next few days were going to play out with him off work and me still hanging about his house. After what had just occurred, was he going to expect sex as commonplace now? We'd need to have a talk about that. It was a one-and-done situation, and he would have to be okay with it. Or I would need to go to a hotel…or back home, which I really, really didn't want to do. The thought terrified me, and I shoved it away.

After I towel-dried my hair and braided it back, I slipped into some jeans, a plain white tee, and my Green Bay Packers sweatshirt. I doubled up on socks, as my feet were freezing on his hardwood floors. I almost considered crawling back into the warmth of the bed, but when I opened the door, Wolf was gone. The smell of breakfast had my stomach growling. I made my way to the kitchen and saw Wolf had three pans on the stove and was cooking away.

He had put his sweatpants on but that was it. No shirt and no socks. How was he not cold? But damn, he did look fine. His smooth, lean, muscular body maneuvered with such ease and confidence. He turned to me upon sensing my presence.

"Good morning. Do you like Spam by chance?" he asked, and I tried to hide my embarrassment as I noticed the vivid bite mark on his shoulder.

"Yeah, actually, I do." Rocky, being from Hawaii, had introduced me to it when we had first started dating. "Thinly sliced and fried is my favorite."

He smiled vibrantly. "Mine, too!"

He had a great smile, with perfect teeth. Either he had been genetically blessed or had worn braces at some point. I had not been genetically blessed, but, luckily, my foster mom had ensured every drop of money she received from the State for caring for me went directly to me and whatever I needed. I had perfect teeth by the time I was fourteen, after only a couple years enduring orthodontist appointments.

I watched Wolf work as I went to his Keurig to make coffee. When I opened the drawer to grab a K-Cup, I saw that there was a dozen different types of coffee, not just the generic kind I'd seen the day before. I looked at him. Gone was the sex god from last night. Back was the sweet, kind, calm, master's-degree nerd cop, chef. Okay, so he still looked like a sex god, but there was no trace of the dirty-talking man who could make me wet by simply commanding it. I grabbed the French-vanilla creamer and poured some into my Christmas coffee mug.

How could he be so confident? Maybe all cops were confident? His gun was sitting on the counter near me. Was he starting to trust me? That was good, right? But also, a little unnerving. Trust was something you built up with friends, not with strangers. You could never really trust a stranger, and that's what we ultimately were—strangers.

He served me up fried eggs, hashbrowns, thinly sliced fried Spam, and berries. God, I could get used to this. His hashbrowns weren't just plain old hashbrowns, either. He had added chopped peppers and onions to them—O'Brien Hashbrowns, he called them.

"So, I got a text from Salone a bit ago. I hope you don't mind, but I explained to Detective O'Dell and Salone yesterday I was in communication with you regarding the case. Salone said they received the medical examiner's report. So hopefully it's not too much longer before the investigation closes."

It would be over soon. A good thing for sure, but my thoughts went back to Rosie. Wolf would be able to wash his hands of me, and Rosie would be well enough to go home.

"This is great news. What's wrong?" Wolf asked me hesitantly.

"No, absolutely, it's just, I'm supposed to pick Rosie up in a few days, and after stepping foot in there last night...I'm just not ready to stay there yet."

Wolf took a bite of Spam. "She can come here." He said it with such ease, like it was no big deal.

"What? No. I can't put you out like that. You don't have dogs, and you've already done so much for me. I'm sure I can find a dog friendly hotel around here." My mind was running a mile a minute.

"Raven, seriously you won't be putting me out. And I do have a dog, but Tiffany got her in the divorce. She is a boxer named Leia." His sadness was tangible.

My previous thoughts pushed aside. "Do you ever get to see her?"

He leaned back in his chair. "No. Tiffany doesn't care to see me and won't answer my calls or texts when I ask about Leia."

"I'm so sorry." *That's what you get for cheating* I wanted to chide, but he looked so sad, I did feel bad for him.

"Thanks, but my point is, I love dogs."

Relief washed over me. He truly was a nice guy. "Seriously? Alright then. I swear we won't hang out here for long," I promised and then took a sip of my coffee.

"Not a problem. You all done?" I nodded as I took the last berry off my plate and popped it into my mouth.

I couldn't help but stare at his arms as he grabbed my plate. Or his back as he turned to bring it to the sink. His skin was flawless. Not even a single tattoo. Just pure perfection. Rocky had been tattooed probably fifty times over, with one full sleeve and one half, and multiple on his chest and thighs and back. He had been perfect, too, but he was gone, and I had to stop thinking about it. I pushed the ideas of Rocky and Sex God Wolf out of my head. I needed a distraction.

I clapped my hands together, and Wolf looked at me with a raised eyebrow.

"So," I said to him, "let's get you finally moved in!"

He cringed slightly but then winked. "I knew you'd motivate me. Alright. Let's go for it."

Chapter Ten

We spent the next three days emptying box after box, hanging paintings and pictures. We did several loads of laundry and drove multiple items to secondhand stores for donation. Wolf insisted on getting rid of most of the décor items—for a fresh start. Who was I to judge, even if most of the items seemed of perfect quality?

We only stopped working for food and when Wolf worked out. I read a book from his collection on the couch down in the basement while he did hardcore circuit trainings in his basement gym setup. I tried to keep my glances to a minimum, but his strength and agility were something to see. He was a natural athlete. Not just strong and fast, but someone who could probably hit a home run, make a three-point shot, and run a timely marathon, all without much practice.

After one of our donation drops, I helped him pick out new décor and a new set of kitchenware to replace his Christmas-themed dishes. Tiffany had kept the rest and given him only the holiday set. We even went mattress and bedroom set shopping for the guest rooms. Wolf wanted one to be more on the feminine side and one to be more masculine for when his niece and nephew stayed over. I liked helping him, and conveniently, we liked the same look: clean and classic, yet cozy with cool tones. Also, keeping busy helped keep my mind off everything else, for the most part. Whenever a thought of that night started to creep in, I'd grab another box, and *poof*, the impending memory vanished and was replaced with thoughts of Wolf and his life. Who he was as a person. It was an excellent distraction.

On the third day, although his truck was loaded up with his recent purchases, I insisted that I treat him to a lunch out. He'd fed me so much already, it was the least I could do. He tried to make excuses to get out of it, saying he would make us food, until finally agreeing, but only if he could pay. I agreed, still planning to pay. We settled on his favorite, O'Ryan's—a bar that apparently had the best sliders and loaded potato skins. I was in at the mention of *potato*.

O'Ryan's Irish Pub was a large establishment. A dark-oak bar extended the entirety of one wall, a dozen barstools perched at it. Irish whiskey and beer promotional posters, mirrors, and lights carefully decorated the entire area, and booths lined the opposite side of the main room before stopping at a dance floor and small stage set for live performances. Further down, off the dance floor, were a few four-tops with chairs and beyond them, pool tables and dart boards. It looked like it would have a fun-filled evening atmosphere.

With it being midday during the middle of the work week, there were only a few patrons enjoying a drink or lunch, and besides the occasional crack of the pool balls, it was quiet. An oddly intimate place for such a seemingly lively environment. I supposed I'd have to come back here in the evening sometime when there was live music. I imagined it was a place no one would question a person on their own. There was even a back patio where I could most likely bring Rosie on warmer days.

We slid into a booth, sitting across from one another.

"Do you want something to drink? Beer or cocktail?" he offered.

"Yeah, I'll take whatever you're having."

He got up, and after a moment chatting with the bartender, he returned with menus under one arm and two frosted glasses of a lighter beer.

"It's a lager. Harp."

"Thank you," I said and took a sip. As with food, I was not picky with my beverages either.

The bartender working the front, who also happened to be the owner of the establishment as Wolf had explained—named Ryan, of course—came to take our order. Wolf ordered the chicken cobb salad, his favorite he'd told me, and I ordered the loaded potato skins.

"So, explain to me where this healthy eating came from. Besides, Spam and alcohol, do you ever have a cheat day?" I asked before sipping my beer.

Wolf's hands were loosely clasped around his glass. "I guess it started in high school. We had a really great weights-and-conditioning teacher at my school. He didn't just have us kids do random weightlifting but really taught us all about our bodies, proper form, agility techniques, as well as the best foods, to keep us lean and cut. I was a three-sport athlete; football, basketball, and track and field. My dad was not really into any of that—my mom had been the athlete-so I just kind of sucked up as much information from my teacher as I could." He unclasped his hands and took a long drink. "It made a difference. I noticed I felt better and had more energy. But don't get me wrong; I love food and love to cook. So to answer your question, I don't necessarily have cheat days, but I do indulge whenever I want. I just don't usually want to indulge, is the thing."

"I see. Well, I wish I didn't want to indulge all the time…but I do," I said with a wink.

He smiled back, and then his face fell serious. "Okay. So, I have a critical question I need to ask you."

I adjusted in my seat, suddenly reminded I was not having lunch with a lifelong friend but a cop I'd only just met. "Shoot," I said, willing myself to sound casual and trying not to cringe at my poor choice of wording.

"If you had to choose, who would you rather be: Samwise Gamgee or Frodo Baggins, and why?" His serious face cracked into a sideways grin, and I felt mine do the same. The last two nights, we had binge watched *The Hobbit* movies, and tonight our plan was to get through *The Lord of the Rings*.

"Hmm well…as far as Hobbits go, in general, I feel I am much more relatable to Merry or Pippin; you know, loving Second Breakfast, Elevenses, and all."

Laughing, Wolf scolded me, "Nope, nope, gotta choose either Sam or Frodo."

"Alright then. Definitely Frodo. I think I'm the type to sacrifice myself for the greater good but would probably need some help along the way." Our food arrived and we thanked Ryan before I turned the question on Wolf. "And you? Frodo or Sam?"

"Well, if you choose Frodo, then I guess I choose Sam."

I'd lifted a bite of potato to my mouth but set it back down. "And why is that?"

"It's like you said, Frodo might need some help along the way, and Sam was that person."

I didn't know how to respond. It was possible I was reading too much into it, but was he saying he was the Sam to my Frodo in some corny but cute way? He was helping me by letting me stay with him, but I was no Frodo.

I lifted my glass. "To Sam!"

"To Frodo!" he announced and lifted his glass, too.

A man at the bar lifted his own glass of beer and shouted, "Go, Pack, Go!" We both snickered and got to our food.

Our conversations flowed easily and comfortably, as they had the prior days, and I ate every single bite of every single potato skin. We kept topics away from the past unless it was regarding experiences in college and mostly chatted about who we were as people now. Our likes and dislikes. Books. Shows we liked and movies. The Green Bay Packers and the Milwaukee Bucks. I avoided childhood topics and our family situations as best I could. He didn't press, but I knew he was aware every time I changed the subject from something I didn't want to get into.

When we returned to his house, I helped him set up the bedframes. We rearranged the guest bedrooms a few times before settling on the final configuration, all the while blaring the best of the '90s and early-2000s music.

We were just finishing up another exceptional homecooked dinner, with *The Lord of the Rings* playing in the background, when Wolf turned to me. "So, tomorrow is Thanksgiving, and I am assuming you don't have any plans?"

I stopped mid-bite. *Shit.* I had forgotten about the whole exchange I'd read between him and his sister. "Umm, yes, you would be right about that." We were sitting in our now usual spots at the table, him at the far end, his back to the wall and window, and me closest to the living room.

His hand lingered on his half-drank beer. "My family always goes to my dad's house, just over in the Hillcrest Heights area—my sister Lauren, her husband, my niece and nephew, and my sister Jillian."

He didn't mention his mom. I guessed either his parents were divorced or his mom had passed away. Over the past three days, I'd done such a good job keeping family out of the topics, I wasn't entirely sure about his own. I knew bits and pieces about his family from seeing pictures we'd unpacked and from our conversation a few nights before, but I'd let on nothing about mine. He probably thought I didn't have any.

"Usually, my Uncle Tommy's whole group is there, too, but they decided on a resort in Mexico this year. So it'll just be a small group tomorrow." He cleared his throat and tipped his beer toward me, "You should come with me."

I swore I heard a slight undertone of vulnerability in his voice but I shook it off. No, he was just being polite.

I felt the disappointment of him leaving me tomorrow hit and set my fork down. I tried to not look how I felt. "Oh, no. I don't want to crash your family gathering. Plus, I didn't really grow up celebrating

Thanksgiving, or really any holidays for that matter, so it's not a big deal for me to be alone on Thanksgiving." Also, I wanted to add, given my native heritage, it would probably be inappropriate for me to celebrate it, but I wasn't even entirely sure about that.

He looked shocked but curious. "You didn't celebrate any holidays? Is it because of your religion?"

"No. I'm not really religious, but that's not why. My foster mom I lived with for the majority of my childhood just didn't celebrate any holidays. I never knew why; she was an old Romanian lady and never ever talked about religion. Sometimes I would celebrate a holiday if I was visiting with friends." I thought about those few years in a row when I'd spent every holiday at my best friend Lilly's house. I didn't want to tell him about her, didn't want to think about her, so I continued, "And when I was with Rocky I did, but I haven't celebrated a holiday since he passed away. So please don't feel bad for me. It's not a big deal. You go have fun with your family. I will just stay here if you are okay with it. What time do you think you'll be back?" I tried to sound nonchalant about it…as if the air in my lungs wasn't about to explode out of me.

"Well, usually we all stay the night out there unless I have to work. I took time off, though. I don't go back to work until Saturday." Panic was starting to set in at the thought of being alone overnight. He must have seen it in my face, because he added, "But I can come back after dinner tomorrow."

My panic eased a bit. "Whatever you feel most comfortable with. I think I could stay the night alone. I'll have to do it eventually anyway, right?"

He looked at me steadily across the table. He had to know I was lying. I was starting to feel like a fucking charity case to this man again. *How embarrassing.* I got up to clear my plate, my cheeks heating.

"This isn't a pity invite, Raven. I want you to come. You deserve to try my turkey and all the other great food that will be there. I'm going to get up at four in the morning to start cooking the turkey, I've had it dethawing in the garage fridge for a few days now. We take holiday food very seriously in the Rivers' household. I know you wouldn't want to miss out on that." He said the last part playfully.

I started to clean up the kitchen and looked over the island at him. He was sitting comfortably, his beer in his hand. He clearly knew food was the way to my heart.

"What would you even tell your family about me?" I sighed.

"I'll just say you're my new friend. They don't need to know details."

Friend? Obviously that wasn't the case, but we had been friendly toward each other—quite friendly. "Alright." I smiled a little uneasily. I really didn't want to be left alone. "I'll go. Can I help you with any of the turkey preparations?"

Wolf shook his head, "Nope." He tipped his beer toward himself. "Remember? Kitchen snob."

I laughed. "But not when someone else is cleaning."

He turned his beer bottle to point at me and smiled. "You're not wrong there." Although, he did get up and help me clean the rest of the kitchen.

Later that night, after we had finished our *Lord of Rings* binge session, we got in his bed. And, just like the past couple nights, we didn't have sex. I didn't ask him to help me forget, and he didn't ask me if I wanted to. There had been no inappropriate talking or touching since the first time I'd asked for it, but I did still find my way into his arms each night.

It was as if it were an unspoken plan of action. It somehow felt as if he needed to hold me as much as I needed him to do it. Maybe he missed his ex or just a warm body to lay next to? I hadn't realized how badly I missed it either until some fuck had to break into my house.

I didn't necessarily care for this sense of need or want. In fact, I had done everything to avoid needing or wanting anybody, especially this past year. But my heart ached for Rocky at times, and it crushed me to linger on that feeling too long. I knew it wasn't smart to let this continue with Wolf, but I couldn't stop it either. I liked his warm, strong body holding mine. I liked feeling safe and comfortable; it eased the ache. I knew—I should stop it, I really should—but I didn't have it in me. So, just like the nights before, I closed my eyes, my head on his chest, and dozed off peacefully.

Chapter Eleven

Wolf hadn't been lying; he took the Thanksgiving turkey very seriously. I awoke to delicious smells wafting into his bedroom, and I scrambled to get out there. I grabbed the sweatshirt he had worn the day before off the edge of his bed, put it on, and swooped my hair into a messy bun. I'd slept in only the Christmas pajama bottoms again and the white tank top, his body warmth more than enough, but damn, he kept his home too cold for me.

I pulled on a pair of socks after using the restroom and made my way out of his room. He had to be tired; we had stayed up so late due to our binge session and he hadn't mentioned the other side dishes, but I remembered from his conversation with his sister he was taking on like three or four. There was no way he didn't need any help.

As I came around the corner to the living room area, the television was on the current football game, and I turned toward the kitchen to see spices and ingredients all over the island. It was by far the messiest I had ever seen his kitchen. On the counter, he had a cup of coffee in one of his new mugs—light blue with a white handle. It was steaming next to a plate with an equally steamy omelet. He smiled at me when I came into the kitchen.

"Perfect timing! I just slid that onto your plate, and the coffee should still be hot, too. I think I put the right amount of creamer in it." He didn't pause from his ministrations with what looked to be his creamed corn dish.

"Wow, thank you! I came out here to see if you needed help with the dishes, but you also made breakfast? Who the hell are you?" I sat down to dig into the omelet.

He flipped a kitchen towel over his shoulder and grinned. "You'll find when I want something, I make it happen." He winked.

Would I? So many times over the past few days, he had made subtle comments like that. Little things, as if we were going to continue to be in each other's lives after this…whole investigation. Obviously, he was sorely mistaken, because I'd hopefully go back to living my normal, quiet life, and he'd go back to his life, which seemed pretty wonderful. I needed to address the elephant in the room before things went too far, but it would have to wait until later because the coffee and omelet were demanding my undivided attention.

After I finished eating the insanely scrumptious breakfast and he'd assured me he didn't want any help, I got dressed quickly and grabbed the last few boxes of items to be dropped off at the donation center and headed out. I wanted to at least be helpful in some way.

While out, I had a slight panic attack realizing it was my first time at a store by myself since the incident and I started to feel paranoid someone was watching me, following me. But then another thought caused me greater panic when I realized I had nothing presentable to wear for Thanksgiving, nor a hostess gift.

Growing up, I'd picked up bits and pieces of what people did for holidays the few times I joined in at friends' houses, or watched holiday movies, but also when I was dating Rocky. Rocky's mom had taught me to always look presentable going to a new place to meet new people and to always bring a hostess gift.

When I thought of Leilani, I sometimes missed her, but then I quickly shoved that feeling out of the way when I remembered how everything had unfolded after Rocky died. I'd decided it was fine to remember the life lessons she'd taught me, but it was another thing to miss her. So, after I dropped off the boxes at the donation center, I stopped at Target and grabbed multiple bottles of wine, not knowing what anyone would like. I then picked out a knee-length black skirt, a silky long-sleeved turquoise blouse that buttoned in the front and tapered at my wrists, and black tights. Then I found some light-brown booties to complete the look.

I stopped at the makeup section and got all my usual products and then went to the minimal jewelry counter. I picked up some gold stud heart earrings, a matching bracelet with one single tiny heart, and a heart ring.

Money had never been an issue for me. My parents had been in their mid-40s when they adopted me. I had been their only child and from what I now knew, being an adult, they had managed to get all their ducks in a row before adopting me. Their house and cars had been paid off and they'd had hefty life insurance policies, let alone savings and 401(k)s. They'd even had the foresight to have me as their sole beneficiary for all of it.

I never knew who at the state had taken care of everything with the sale of the house and cars, but when I was close to turning eighteen years old, my social worker, Brenda, picked me up one day and took me to lunch. She sat me down and explained all about my money. She had me go to financial classes, and she set me up with a financial advisor to ensure I understood what to do with that amount of money. Brenda was a saint and one of the few people I still kept in contact with from time to time; probably the only living person in this entire world I could honestly say I trusted.

When I got back to Wolf's, the kitchen was clean, and he was in the guest bathroom shower. I quickly slipped into his bathroom to take my own shower. I imagined we still had a while before we needed to head out, so I decided to actually take my time putting makeup on and drying my hair. I left it down.

Down, my hair went all the way to my lower back. When I undid the packet of tights, I realized I had accidentally grabbed thigh highs, each ending in a lacy finish. They were cute but way too sexy for an evening meeting people for the first time. Luckily, when I slipped on the skirt, I could see no one would be able to tell they weren't regular tights. I tucked in my blouse, put the jewelry on, and stepped back to check myself in the mirror.

I looked vibrant! I looked good! I looked like my long-lost self. The eye makeup I'd applied made my green eyes pop. It had been so long since I had purposefully tried to look nice, because I hadn't needed to. Or maybe I just hadn't cared or wanted to impress anyone. Not that I was trying to impress anyone now. I was likely never going to see Wolf's family again. Probably never see Wolf again after this whole fiasco was over. I sighed and walked out to the living room.

Wolf had taken the turkey out of the oven and placed it on a large serving platter, wrapping tin foil over it. He looked so nice in black slacks and a buttoned-up green knitted sweater; it had a large collar that laid flat against his collarbones. He heard my boots approaching and said, "So, turkey is done, and I've got everything else pa—" he stopped talking and did a double take when he looked at me. "…packed and ready to go," he finished. "Did you buy new clothes?"

"I did. I stopped off at the store while I was out. I got a shit ton of wine, too. Your family drinks wine, right?"

"Yeah, they do. Total winos actually. You look really nice." His eyes lingered on my face.

I hated compliments—never knew what to say or do. I always felt awkward. A memory of Rocky popped into my head. Of him kissing me all over and after each kiss, giving me a compliment. I took a deep breath and pushed it away.

"Thanks and same to you. I love your sweater." I could feel my cheeks heating so I turned to break his stare. "Let me help get the door for you."

We loaded up the car with all the food Wolf had prepared and our overnight bags of clothes and toiletries. If I hadn't felt weird about staying at a cop's house before, I definitely did now. What was I thinking, going to spend the holiday with a stranger and his whole family? I knew the answer: my need for not being alone outweighed the awkward situation I was putting myself in.

Once we settled into Wolf's truck, he turned the radio to the football game, and we headed off to his dad's place. "Sorry, did you want to listen to music at all? It's just a habit of mine to turn on the game, but we can listen to music instead." Always so damn thoughtful, wasn't he?

"No, I'm good. I like hearing it in the background."

We cruised down the road for a couple minutes before I asked, "So your dad's not married? You don't have an evil stepmom or anything I have to worry about meeting?"

He chuckled. "Nope. My dad has been a widower for twenty-five years now."

So not a divorce then and not an absentee mom. She'd been taken from him, and it sounded like at a really tough age to lose your mom. My heart hurt for him. I had been two when I lost my birth mom, and still very young when I'd lost my adoptive parents. I had vague memories of being sad about them. I had only been six, but I knew they had loved me, and I loved them. I remembered that feeling—the feeling of love and safeness, of laughing, and smiles. I remembered my adoptive dad being funny and making me laugh but I couldn't remember an actual joke he'd told or what I would laugh about. I remembered my adoptive mom singing to me and rubbing my back at night, but I couldn't remember the songs. I couldn't remember a single conversation I'd had with them, and that hurt. So, to be 10 years old when you lost a parent…I couldn't imagine. I just couldn't imagine. "I'm sorry you lost your mom."

He didn't say anything, just took his right hand off the steering wheel and lightly squeezed my knee. I couldn't help it, I placed my hand over his, trapping it there. He loosened his hand and let it curve to the top of my knee, and I didn't try to pull away. It was too much, too much like what a couple in a relationship would do, but I didn't stop it.

"So, you're telling me your dad never remarried. What about dating?" I said to keep the conversation going instead of having an awkward, sad silence.

"Nope, and he's never shown any interest. Even when we've told him he should, he refuses. He says, 'What's the point? No one would want an old geezer like me.' We know it's just an excuse. He still talks to my mom. Like out loud, as if she were here and could hear him. He asks her questions and has always kept her in his conversations."

"Is that hard for you?" I asked, curious.

"My sisters hated it at first. I think because it was so raw after she'd died so suddenly. I remember Lauren yelling at him early on to stop it because it hurt too much, but he sat us down and told the three of us he would never stop and that we shouldn't either. That too often, people lose the most important people in their lives and stop talking, stop thinking about them because it hurts too much, and all it does is make the person fade away eventually, which is disrespectful to the love they gave while they were here with us."

Flashes of pictures of my birth mom I had seen on the reservation popped into my head, of the few family pictures I had of me as a child with the smiling faces of my adoptive parents, of Lilly, Mama Elena, and Rocky. I had done that. I had forced myself to stop thinking about them as much as possible. I had tried to outrun and outlive that life of loss. What had it done, but exactly what Wolf's dad said it would? Fade their memory—and is that what I wanted? I wanted to forget the hurt, but had I wanted to forget them—or the idea of them, in my parents' case?

Wolf looked at me. "Are you okay?"

I nodded. "Yeah. I just think your dad is really wise." I smiled. "And I'm sure any old granny would be lucky to snag your dad up if he's anything like you."

Wolf smiled back. "You're not wrong."

"If you don't mind me asking, how did your mother pass away?"

He frowned and shook his head. "No, I don't mind. She was a victim of a mall shooting." His voice made a slight crack as he spoke. I sucked in a breath. "I was in the fifth grade, and my parents had taken the day off work to get some Christmas shopping done while us kids were in school."

I stroked my thumb over his hand, which was still cupped on my knee. "Did your dad get shot?"

"No. Actually, a couple of years ago, my dad got really drunk one Christmas Eve. We were out in his garage messing with his old car, and he just broke down to me. He told me he had been with my mom the entire time at the mall, and then he had left her to go check something out at Radio Shack. You remember that store? Anyway, he was at Radio Shack when the shooting happened at the other end of the mall where my mom was. He was bawling on the garage floor, telling me about how much he regretted leaving her to go see something he wanted. It hadn't even been for one of us kids. He was being selfish, he said. He went through several different what-ifs and maybe-I-could-haves. Told me he should have been there to push her out of the way, or maybe he could have covered her body with his. He went over this scenario and that scenario. I think that was the last time I cried, to be honest. My dad and I, on the garage floor, hugging and crying. I just felt so bad for him. My mom had been gone for so many years, and this man had been carrying around this guilt for all this time." Wolf shook his head.

I thought maybe his eyes were shining a little more than usual.

"I guess most people in that type of situation would feel the same thing he did," Wolf continued. "It just sucks he's dealt with it for so long and will continue to do so. I don't even know if he remembers telling me, I mean, the man was really wasted. I'd never seen him that drunk before. But I hope he does remember. I hope it helped him to get it off his chest. Here I am with a master's degree in psychology, and I don't even know what to say to my own dad to help with his grief."

I squeezed his hand. "You don't specialize in grief counseling, Wolf, and him just talking about it with you, even if he doesn't remember, I am sure it helped." I tried to shove the thoughts of my own guilt about Rocky aside. A different situation, but multiple what-ifs and different scenarios always played through my head. Had he ever complained of chest pain, and I'd brushed it off? What if I'd woken up in the middle of the night and noticed he was struggling or had stopped breathing? Maybe I could have saved him. I could 100 percent understand that part of what Wolf's dad was going through.

"I know," he sighed, "but I can only imagine how he feels. I was just 10, and it was so long ago, but it's wild how some days, it hurts just like we lost her yesterday. You know?"

And I did, with Rocky and with Lilly, at least. I did. "Yes. I know," I said quietly.

Lilly, my best friend for five years, the most impressionable years for a preteen/teen girl, had died by taking her own life during our junior year of high school. The girl who at age twelve spent hours and hours creating a PowerPoint presentation and speech to her parents about why they should adopt me and make me her sister. She had been my family. I knew that now. She hadn't been just a friend but my chosen family. The regret I felt for Lilly was different than for Rocky. We had been inseparable, and I'd known her, really known her, so how had I not known she was suffering? But I hadn't. The day before she did it, we'd been shopping for our prom dresses, the boys we'd wanted to ask us had, and everything seemed so perfect. I remember being so happy that day trying on those dresses. There were so many smiles and laughs with her mom as we tried on dress after dress, giggling hysterically. Her dad had found her the next day in her bedroom when she didn't come down for breakfast. An overdose on painkillers she'd found in her parents' medicine cabinet from a past surgery. Even after all this time, thinking about her made my heart hurt and my eyes burn.

Yes, I knew exactly what Wolf meant. I must have been squeezing his hand, because he stroked my knee with his thumb and said, "Do you want to talk about it?"

Well, that had gotten depressing fast. I didn't want that. I wanted light and easy. I didn't want this happy, seemingly carefree man to be sad about his mom, and I didn't want to even go there with my thoughts about Lilly. I took a breath. "Nope. I'm good. I think I do want some music, though."

"Go for it." He moved his hand back to the steering wheel as I moved mine off his to change the radio station.

Chapter Twelve

We jammed out to 80s rock the rest of the ride. I'd learned from the previous days Wolf had a surprisingly great voice and zero confidence issues, which gave me the courage to go along with it. I wasn't as familiar with the songs and we were dying with laughter by the time we pulled up to his dad's house, by my near-constant wrongly sung lyrics. I hadn't let myself be silly like that in so long and it felt good.

"Sorry, I'm a 90s baby! I did the best I could." I shrugged.

"Are you kidding? You did great! I loved it."

We each had our arms full of items as we approached the opening front door. A handsome older man wearing a cream-colored cable-knit sweater and light-colored slacks greeted us.

"There you are!"

"Hi, Dad!"

"I'm not talking to you, son! I'm talking to that turkey! I've been dreaming about it all day!" said the man with a Tweety Bird expression. He then chuckled at his own joke.

Wolf shook his head smiling. "Wait no longer! Dad, this is Raven, my friend I told you would be joining us. Raven, this is my dad, Jim."

"Hello, Raven! I'm so happy you are here! We usually have such a big crew, so the more the merrier!" We awkwardly shook hands as I balanced multiple items.

"Thanks for having me. I selfishly just wanted to try Wolf's turkey, so really I do appreciate the invite."

Jim laughed. "Oh, well, I don't blame you, and you won't be disappointed, my dear. My boy can cook a mean turkey! Let me help you all with some of this. Come on in!"

He grabbed the bird from Wolf with exaggerated eager eyes that made me smile, and Wolf took some items from me before we wandered into his childhood home.

The two men led the way to the kitchen, and we set down all the food on the counter.

"Why don't you give this young lady a tour before it gets a little busy with everyone showing up?" Jim nudged his son.

"Great idea. We can grab the bags on the way up," Wolf told me and we started to head back down the hall before he lightly pulled me back around and pointed.

His finger led me to Jim who was lifting the foil off the turkey.

"Hey now, no sneaking!"

Jim jumped at his son's voice and tsked. "Ah, you caught me!"

"I know you old man!" Wolf laughed.

Jim shoved the foil back down and waved us on. "I'll be good. Maybe…" he made no promises.

Jim Rivers' home was beautiful. Wolf explained the large house had been built in 1993, and the Rivers family had been the first and only owners. It had been his mother's dream home he said and I could see why. The front sitting room off to the right of the foyer included a cozy wood-burning fireplace with a fire currently crackling and a gorgeous black piano in the corner. The hallway, which ran along the side of the staircase, led down to the open-concept kitchen and dining room where we had offloaded the food. The dining room consisted of a massive wood table in front of huge floor-to-ceiling windows which sandwiched French doors. These opened to the backyard, which looked out to a large fenced-in yard and beyond that, an expanse of flat landscape and, even farther out, a forest of trees. To the right of the dining area there was another living room, also consisting of a crackling fire and another gorgeous fireplace. Jim chimed in he'd opened up the walls and completely revamped the downstairs kitchen and dining space five years earlier. The kitchen seemed out of a

French Riviera magazine with beautiful stonework in creamy browns and rustic reds.

After the downstairs tour, Wolf grabbed our overnight bags and led me upstairs to the bedrooms, one of which we put our things into.

"We'll stay in here. There's a Jack and Jill bathroom shared with the next bedroom over. My niece usually stays in that one." I couldn't determine if he was telling me so I knew nothing could go down tonight or so I would remember to lock the bathroom door.

The space was small but quaint, and although there was a queen size bed taking up the majority of the space, it was Wolf who seemed too large and out of place for the little room.

"If you can believe it, this used to be my room, before my dad changed it to the *Antiques Roadshow*." He grabbed up a tchotchke off an ornate corner shelf and showed it me. "Like, what even is this?"

I laughed. "No clue. But at least he has some decorating talent. Unlike his son." I joked.

He set the object back to its spot and placed his hands over his chest in mock pain, "Ouch! I just needed a little help was all," he winked at me.

He showed me the rest of the bedrooms and let me know where people would or usually slept. I hadn't been on a tour of someone's home like this before, but I guessed it was a normal thing to do when staying the night at a new place. It seemed like an invasion of privacy, if you asked me.

The other three rooms he showed were similar to the first; small, clean, and nicely kept. The home had a mature, classic vibe to it, but it smelled fresh and new.

Lastly, he showed me his dad's room, which was at the end of the hall toward the back of the house. It was by far the largest of the bedrooms, and I wondered if he thought of his mom when he looked at it. If he remembered being a child and running into his parents' room—to her—when he was scared or sick. I remembered doing that once with Mama Elena when I'd woken up not feeling well one night; it had to have been early on when I'd first started staying with her. She'd told me I couldn't sleep in her bed, it wasn't appropriate, but she'd held my hand and brought me back to my own bed. She ended up bringing in a chair and sitting there until I fell asleep.

Mama Elena had not been a warm-and-fuzzy sort of lady by any means, but she'd been kind enough and had taken care of me in the only way she knew how—a way I was certain was a hundred times better than how she was treated as a child. She brought me soup, medicine, and tissues when I was sick, and took me to my medical and dental appointments until I was old enough to drive myself.

She took very good care of all the foster babies that came through her home up until I became the one getting up with them in the middle of the night and early in the mornings more often than not. She was just simply getting too old and too tired, seeing as how I had come to live with her when she was already in her late 60's.

After my adoptive parents passed away and it was clear none of their family members wanted to take me in, I was sent to Mama Elena's house for only a few days. She was a respite foster care parent for babies, which meant she only took in infants and babies for short periods until they went to long-term foster care homes. I was already older than any child she usually would have for respite, but for whatever reason, I was placed there until I could be placed in another home. I stayed with her for a week until they found a long-term home for me. After only a couple weeks at the long-term home, I begged Brenda to let me go back to Mama Elena's. The foster dad was creepy, and from what I could remember, nothing had happened, other than the way he looked at me wasn't right, and the foster mom was mean to me because of it. Brenda had worked her magic and somehow convinced the older woman to take me in long-term, and I never had to see those people again.

The sounds of more arrivals floated upstairs. "That would be my sister Lauren and her crew," Wolf said, and we made our way back down to the foyer for introductions.

Lauren Hill, a tall, beautiful, curly-haired brunette with brown eyes and a heart-shaped face, smiled at me as she shook my hand. "So good to meet you, Raven. This is my husband, Drew, and our kids, Sara and Devon." I shook their respective hands. I was very happy I had cleaned myself up and bought the new outfit. The entire Hill family had dressed nicely for their Thanksgiving holiday—Sara and Lauren in matching green dresses with black lace edges, Devon in black slacks and a blue sweater, and Drew in a nice green polo with a Green Bay Packers emblem in the left corner with khaki slacks.

Drew was shorter than Lauren and his teenage son by a couple inches, with short black hair and dark-brown eyes. His skin was brown like mine, darker even. Both Devon and Sara had a lighter skin tone than their dad but shades darker than their mom. Devon was at least six-foot-two and had a kind face like his mom but with striking blue eyes. He looked a little embarrassed when we shook hands.

Sara, who looked about 8 years old, had long, dark curls and dark sparkling eyes with a sprinkling of freckles across her cheeks. "You're so pretty, and I love your blouse. Oh! Your nails aren't painted! Can I paint your nails?" she said to me, her eyes wide. Everyone laughed at her breathless excitement.

"Sara, how about we get unloaded first before we pounce on Uncle Wolf's friend with questions and salon tips and tricks?" her father offered.

"Okaaay," Sara whined.

Wolf had scooped both kids into big hugs, but he kept his hands on Devon's shoulders. They were nearly at eye level, but Wolf still had a couple inches on him, "Hey, bud. I'm sorry I missed your game the other night. How'd it go?"

Devon came to life then, explaining how the starting shooting guard got hurt in the first quarter and he got put in.

"You're starting on varsity now?" Wolf's voice was full of awe.

Lauren cut in then. "Yes, he is! He was incredible, Wolf. He scored sixteen points, made all his free-throws, six rebounds, and eight assists."

"Well, the other team was shitty," Devon said, looking a little embarrassed from his mom's praise.

"Language!" Sara scolded her brother, and Drew rolled his eyes before giving his son a pointed look.

"Sorry," Devon shrugged.

"Let's get all this stuff upstairs, you guys. Grab some things, please!" Drew said, and he and the kids headed up to the rooms to offload their bags while Wolf, Lauren, and I went to the kitchen to unload their food.

The dining room was already set up with fancy-looking plates, silverware, and glassware. It was like a scene out of a movie, so picturesque and special.

"Dad, this looks beautiful, as usual." Lauren went over and gave her dad a kiss and hug.

"Thanks, hon. I had a little help from your mom this morning. She reminded me to take out the good plates." Jim looked wistfully down at the plate he was carefully positioning.

I was thankful Wolf had mentioned how Jim talked to his wife's spirit, but not wanting to make it obvious, I decided to see if I could be of any assistance with anything.

"What can I do to help, Jim? Wolf refuses to accept my help in the kitchen at his house, other than to clean, and I just want something to do. Please, feel free to put me to work!" I said, looking from Jim to Lauren. I didn't miss the glance Lauren threw Wolf's way, or him deliberately turning away from it. I apparently had said too much. But friends went to friends' houses—it shouldn't have seemed that odd.

"Oh no dear, you are a guest in this house. You just relax and enjoy." Jim smiled at me.

"Actually," Lauren said, "if you can pop open one of those bottles of wine you so thoughtfully brought and pour a few glasses, that would be a great help!"

"On it!" I chirped.

Wolf laughed seeing how excited I was. Having something to do instead of standing awkwardly was amazing. Lauren handed me a corkscrew and brought over five of the wine glasses from the table Jim had set. I popped a bottle of one of the reds and poured the glasses as evenly as I could. I had just started to pass them out when Drew came down the stairs.

I handed him a glass, and he gladly took it. "Are you a mind reader? Thank you!"

I handed one to Jim, and he thanked me as well.

"I'm glad you are all wine drinkers. I took a shot in the dark at what might be a good drink of choice." I hadn't asked Wolf before purchasing, and I hadn't seen any wine at his house. Nor had he drunk any since I'd been staying with him, but people always seemed to drink wine in the movies at holiday dinners.

Wolf took a sip of his wine and smirked. "Just wait until you meet Jill. It's a good thing you bought a lot."

Just then, the sound of the front door opening carried down the hall along with a loud, "Helloooo. I'm heeere! Where are my baaabies?"

"Speaking of…" Lauren said and then pointed up toward the ceiling. Thunderous steps came from up above and the pounding of feet on the stairs had us all grinning.

"Aunt Jilly's here!" Sara's voice screeched excitedly.

Wolf set down his wine, and I followed him down the hall.

When we reached the foyer, Sara was hugging a stunningly beautiful blonde woman. Devon came down the last step and moved into Jill's now open arms.

"Devon! Did you grow another foot since I saw you the other week?"

He shrugged. "Probably."

She handed him a gift bag and shimmied off her brown trench coat. "Let me know if any of this doesn't fit then, and I'll exchange it for you."

He smiled. "Thanks, Aunt Jilly!"

Sara squealed. "Presents?"

"Of course you get presents!" Jillian handed a bag to Sara before looking up at Wolf. "What, did Uncle Wolfie not bring you anything?"

Wolf laughed. "Give me a break! It's not like it's Christmas! Always gotta show me up, huh?" He walked over and gave her a hug then picked up some of the food-storage containers she had set down.

Jillian had somehow carried in two containers of food, four bags, and a bottle of wine. How had she opened the door?

Wolf scowled as he looked through the glass of one of the containers and shouted down the hall, "Lauren! I told you I was going to make the creamed corn!"

Lauren's voice trailed from the kitchen, "I told her you would! She didn't care!"

Jillian wore a satisfied smirk on her face and crossed her arms over her chest. "You know my creamed corn recipe is better than yours, and when I heard we were having a guest—" she looked at me with the same dazzling blue eyes and the same bright smile as Wolf "—I decided we would have an unbiased judge of whose dish is better. I'm Jillian, by the way."

She hung her coat on the rack near the entryway table and came toward me.

"This is Raven, and she's *my* friend. Therefore, she will be biased," Wolf provoked.

I switched my glass of wine to my left hand, anticipating a handshake. "Nice to meet you, Jillian. Just blindfold me, and I will tell the honest-to-God truth." I reached out my hand, but she opened her arms wide and moved toward me.

"I'm a hugger, Raven. I must have my fifteen hugs a day." She was warm and smelled of rosewater and lavender. She released me, and I about had a panic attack trying to keep my glass of red wine as far from her exquisite white knitted long-sleeved dress as I could.

"She's not just saying that, either. She really is a hugger. Like…a lot," Wolf said.

Fifteen hugs a day? I didn't think I'd ever in my life had fifteen hugs in one day, let alone five. I liked her though, and her hug had felt nice. Even though we were perfect strangers, it felt caring; intentional, but in a truly selfless, feel-good way.

"It's so toasty in here. I'm guessing Dad has a fire going in both fireplaces?" She curved her body to look in the front sitting room with the beautiful brick fireplace.

"Of course. In fact, I need to put some more wood in for him," Wolf said.

Sara and Devon had the contents of their gift bags spread throughout the room, with Sara oohing and aahing at the clothes and hair accessories. Both kids thanked their aunt and Devon assured Jillian the clothes would fit—maybe for a week, but they were the right size currently. The aunt dynamic looked good on Jillian; the love the kids had for her and for Wolf was pure.

A wave of yearning went through me. I knew I wouldn't get the chance to be an auntie to anyone.

After I insisted on helping Wolf replenish the fires with wood, we all moved into the dinning room.

Drew, Lauren, and Jim transferred all the food onto platters and bowls that matched the set of plates on the table. Bottles of wine with the corks already popped had been set on either end of the table. Jillian had already poured herself a glass and was filling up Jim's glass with a red. He said he'd have one more glass with dinner and then that was it; that someone needed to stay sober in case of an emergency.

Wolf directed all of us to take a seat as he started to slice up the turkey. Jim sat at one end of the table with Lauren to his left and Drew next to her, and then Sara. I stayed back a little, acting very interested in the pictures on Jim's fridge, until everyone had taken their seats. Jillian had sat to the right of her dad with Devon next to her, so that left a seat next to Devon at the other end of the table. I grabbed my almost empty glass of wine and took my seat next to Devon.

Sure enough, there were already two separate bowls of creamed corn right in front of my plate. Jim started passing food around as conversation flowed easily regarding Devon and Sara's next events. Sara was apparently in musical theater, which I thought suited her well, as she seemed so vibrant.

"Sara will be in this year's performance of *The Dancing Nutcracker*," Lauren informed the room. "I'll send you all the link for tickets. Wolf, there will be four showings, so hopefully your schedule will allow for you to make it to one of them. She's one of the Sugar Plum Fairies!"

Jillian squealed in excitement. "Sara! That's wonderful! I can't wait to see you! I'm going to go to every performance!"

Sara beamed with a bite of roll in her cheek.

Wolf came over with the turkey sliced and passed the tray to me. There was white and dark meat to choose from. I chose one slice of white and one of dark, I did already have a slice of Jim's ham on my plate, but I had to know if this turkey was all it was cracked up to be. I also had a mound of mashed potatoes with gravy, a heap of brussels sprouts with bacon that looked delightful, both of the creamed corns, green-bean casserole, and two rolls with melting butter. Everything was still hot and ready to eat.

These people sure know how to do a holiday!

Wolf replenished our wine glasses as he said, "Very exciting, Sara! I'll make sure I can go to one. I bet you will be the best of the fairies."

Sara smiled enormously, now with a full bite of creamed corn in her mouth. "That's the truth!" We all laughed. She was forward and purposefully silly, and it was adorable.

Chapter Thirteen

The food was to die for. I had never had such an amazing home-cooked meal in my entire life. The turkey truly was out of this world, the flavors were spot on, and I did end up grabbing another slice. If anyone noticed how much I could pack away into my tiny body, nobody said anything. Wolf, having fed me the last few days, already knew about my healthy appetite, but I was pretty positive I ate more than the growing teenage boy beside me.

I was on my fourth glass of wine and feeling extremely gluttonous and happy when Jillian leaned her head down and asked, "Well? Which creamed corn was better? The one from the smaller bowl or the one from the larger?"

I had taken a mental note of where I had put the scoop from each type of bowl on my plate. Everyone now looked at me, waiting expectantly, their faces all in some form of a smile or smirk.

Wolf leaned back in his chair and crossed his arms.

"For starters, let me just say that the entire meal was absolutely amazing, and you all did an incredible job. Thank you so much for having me."

"Hear, hear! And we are so glad you came." Jim lifted his glass. Everyone concurred.

"Now for the winner of this year's creamed-corn competition…" I looked to Sara and then Devon. "Drumroll, please?" They both giggled and started pounding their hands on the table. Drew, Lauren, and Jim all joined in as Jillian and Wolf smirked smugly at one another. "This was extremely close, but I have to give it to…the smaller bowl!"

Wolf was out of his chair whooping before I knew what happened. "Let's go! Let's go!"

Jillian put her hands in her face in defeat but was laughing at the same time.

Wolf made his way over to her. "Can't compete, little sis! Can't compete!" He grabbed her shoulders and squeezed affectionately.

She tipped her head up at him and grinned. "Yeah, well, she must have known it was yours!"

I hadn't known, but seeing Wolf's reaction, I was glad I had chosen his. He was funny and lively, and he made me want to be the same.

"I'm sorry, Jillian! I swear, they were both so good."

She smiled at me. "Yeah, yeah…so much for not being biased!"

Wolf gestured to the table. "How about we do a full vote then, since Jillian thinks Raven is only picking mine because we're friends?"

There were multiple groans of protest, and then Drew spoke up for the masses. "I think we will pass on that little sibling rivalry poll." He leaned back in his seat and put a hand on his stomach.

Everyone, full and happy, began rising from their seats. I moved to start grabbing plates, but Drew stopped me. "Nope. Kids have got it."

Devon and Sara protested, but Drew said, "You guys know the drill."

"But, Dad, this year it's just Sara and me. We normally have at least six others to help." I knew he was referring to cousins from Wolf's uncle's group.

"True, but you also have less plates and food since there are less people, as you so wonderfully pointed out, so the level of clean-up evens out."

Drew grabbed his wine glass and a bottle of red off the table. Devon didn't seem happy about his dad's logic but realized he wasn't getting out of it and started clearing the table. I stayed back with Wolf and helped the kids clear the table before Lauren pulled us away into the adjoining living room with the other grand fireplace to watch the football game. Jim had just added more wood and was stoking it with the poker.

It was a gorgeous room with deep greens and pastel florals and oversized leather couches and armchairs. One whole wall was lined with bookshelves stuffed with books, VHSs, DVDs, CDs, board games, and puzzles—a small glimpse into Wolf and his siblings' childhood. Behind one of the couches, there was a large circular table that looked as if it doubled as a poker table.

We all contentedly watched the game, and before long, Jim was bringing in slices of pie and ice cream for everyone. Everybody exclaimed they were still too stuffed, but we all managed to eat every last bite. I was truly blown away with how Wolf's family could make such delicious meals from scratch.

After the kids finished cleaning, they sat with Jim, who had made them hot chocolates and turned on the movie *Elf*—a tradition, Sara told me. The rest of us moved to the front sitting room for further drinking and music, the football game on mute in the corner. Lauren and Drew peppered me with questions about myself.

"What tribe are you from, Raven?" Drew asked.

I hadn't expected my heritage to come up, but clearly, Drew could tell just by looking at me that I had indigenous blood. I felt Wolf's gaze burning into me as he awaited my answer. He knew basic things about me and had asked safe questions the last few days—since we had spent nearly every waking moment together—but I'd been careful about my choice of words and had not explained to him what had brought me out to Wisconsin.

"I'm not. Well, I do have Rain Tree heritage, but I'm not a tribal member. It's complicated. I was adopted out when I was very young, shortly after my adoptive parents and I moved to California."

I had only learned about my native roots after Mama Elena died. When I'd gone through her stuff to get things in order to sell, I'd found a forgotten box that must've come with me when I was a little kid. In it were letters between my adoptive mother and my maternal grandmother. My adoptive mom had been searching for my roots. They'd been planning a future visit with my birth mother's family who lived on the Rain Tree Reservation, in a letter dated only a month before their accident.

Drew nodded, understanding I was not going to be able to share insight on a culture I knew nothing about. "Ahh. I see. A Lost Bird. I'm sorry to hear that," he said sadly.

I'd never heard the term, Lost Bird before. But it's sure how I felt. "Are you indigenous?" I asked.

"Oh you know, Great Grandma was a Cherokee Princess," Drew laughed.

Again, Drew was making a comment as if I should know what he meant, but I didn't. Luckily, Lauren nudged him. "Yes, he is."

"Jokes aside, my dad is Cherokee but no I don't believe my great grandma was a princess. My mom has Chickasaw blood. Myself and the kids are enrolled Cherokee though. Hey, I wonder if you're enrolled Rain Tree. I don't know their process—every tribe is different but maybe when you were a baby you were enrolled. You should look into that. I can help if you like," Drew offered.

"Oh I never thought of that. I'll let you know," I told him. But I knew it was something I would not be looking into. There was no way I was going back to the reservation. Ever.

But now, with Lord only knows how many glasses of wine I'd drunk, my filter had been lifted. I told them about my time in foster care with Mama Elena and all the babies I had helped take care of with her. How she'd let me stay with her even though she usually only took in infants. I even started to choke up a bit when I spoke of her passing my freshman year of college.

"She sounds like she was a saint," Lauren said kindly. "I can't imagine taking care of babies at that age. It could not have been easy. Seems she was just as lucky to have you as you were to have her." I hadn't really thought of Mama Elena as a saint, but that's what she'd been. By letting me come live with her, she had saved me from nightmares I didn't even want to think about. And although she hadn't been a touchy-feely or outwardly loving person toward me, I knew she'd cared for me. I hoped she'd known how deeply grateful I was for her.

Lauren tipped the last of the wine into my glass.

"Thank you. Seriously, though, enough about me. If I talk anymore, I'll be crying in the bathroom, and Wolf won't invite me back here. Tell me, what do you all do for a living?"

Wolf laughed but I didn't miss the sparkle in his eyes at my mention of coming back here one day. It was obvious it had been my charming way of changing the subject, right? Surely he knew I didn't actually plan on coming back, and that this visit was only happening because of the situation we'd found ourselves in.

Luckily, the conversation did move off the topic of my woeful life, and I learned Lauren and Drew lived in nearby De Pere and worked for the West De Pere school district. Lauren was a fifth-grade teacher, and Drew was an assistant principal at the high school his son went to. Poor Devon; I figured that couldn't be easy.

Jillian lived in Appleton where she was an assistant professor at Lawrence University with her focus in piano.

"That's incredible," I said, and I meant it. "Will you play something?" I motioned to the ancient but elegant-looking piano near the wall by the front window.

"Sure!" She jumped up from her seat, her long golden hair swaying.

Lauren chuckled. "She's always up for a chance to show off."

I had never been musically inclined; my musical journey had been limited to the recorder in the third grade, but I was always delighted for those with natural or hard-earned musical talent.

She started with a piece I was familiar with, I guessed it was Mozart or another classical composer. She was magical. Watching her hands float over the keys was hypnotic. She wasn't an assistant professor at Lawrence University for nothing.

I stood the closest to her to watch, the rest still sitting enjoying the music. She then moved into some more recent pieces from the past decade and started singing. I was blown away by her voice as well.

At one point, Drew grabbed Lauren, and they started dancing. Wolf was laughing at them as they stumbled around the room grinning, and he chimed in every so often to harmonize with Jillian as she sang. Then she switched to an upbeat "Santa Clause Is Coming to Town" and Sara came running in and leaped into her dad's arms. He swung her around while Lauren started grabbing the empty wine glasses from around the room. She had the look of someone who was ready for bed after a long day.

"Alright Sara, say goodnight and then let's get up to bed," Lauren yawned the words out when Jillian finished her last note.

"Oh no please. Please just a few more Christmas songs!" Sara begged.

"There will be plenty of time for that tomorrow. You heard Mom. Say goodnights and up to bed," Drew urged.

"Oh, fine. Goodnight Uncle Wolf. Goodnight Raven." Sara wrapped her arms around Wolf's waist and hugged him tightly.

Wolf leaned down and whispered something in Sara's ear as he hugged her. Sara snickered and then snorted with laughter.

"Don't rile her up more than she already is Wolf," Lauren chastised. "Let's go. Up to bed."

Sara slowly and dramatically turned to Jillian who was still sitting on the piano bench but faced toward the room now.

"I'll be up in a few. Don't hog all the covers like last time," Jillian told Sara and gave her a smile.

We all watched as Sara slowly crept her way to the stairs. She moved at turtle speed. While the rest of us looked on in amusement, her mother and father looked on in unfazed and unimpressed fashion. Which led me to believe this was a usual antic by Sara. It made her all the more endearing to me and I had to stifle a laugh.

Halfway up the stairs Sara stopped and turned with a look of horror. "Raven! I didn't get to paint your nails. Can I tomorrow?"

Wolf looked at me grinning.

"Absolutely! I've been needing a manicure!"

Her tired smile warmed my heart, and she headed upstairs, now at a normal pace. Drew wished everyone goodnight and headed up after her.

Devon and Jim also popped their heads in and gave their goodnights as they sauntered up the stairs after the others.

Lauren returned from dropping off a couple of the wine glasses in the kitchen and squeezed my arm affectionately. "It was great meeting you. I hope you sleep well. We'll see you in the morning."

She told her brother and sister goodnight and went up to attend to the evening routine I was sure young families had.

Jillian left her seat at the piano and announced she'd be getting in her pajamas but promised she would be back down before eventually sharing the room with Sara. Which left me and Wolf still in the room, our wine glasses now empty as there probably wasn't a drop more to be had in this house. With six adults all drinking wine, we had gone through every bottle.

I sat on the couch next to the fire, and Wolf sat next to me, pulling a blanket over our laps.

"Your sister plays beautifully. Can you play at all?"

He nodded. "We all took lessons as kids. I can play a little still, but not anything like Jilly. We joke about her bragging, but honestly, it's always us bragging about her. She's truly a philosopher of the piano. If you hadn't asked her to play, one of us would have before long." Wolf looked at our wine glasses. "I know we are out of wine, but I do make a damn good hot chocolate. Would you like some?"

I hadn't had hot chocolate in years. "That sounds really great, actually."

Wolf stood up, the blanket sliding off him. "Marshmallows and Baileys?"

I smiled up at him. "Absolutely. I like your take on hot chocolate." He grinned back and grabbed our empty wine glasses.

Jillian walked down the stairs in a silky pink pajama set. "Your famous hot chocolate? Make me one too, please!" And then she made herself comfy right where Wolf had been sharing a blanket with me. She looked like a real-life Barbie with her beautiful blonde hair and pink outfit.

"I had planned to, and *I* was sitting there," Wolf said as he walked out of the room.

"You didn't *tap tap*!" she called after him and then looked at me. "Sooo…tell me everything before he gets back! What's your guys' deal?"

I would have choked on my drink had I had one. I wasn't prepared for that much bluntness, but it was a valid question. "Umm, what do you mean? We are just friends. New friends, at that."

"Oh, please! Give me a break! There is no way two gorgeous people like yourselves are just friends."

I chuckled a little; he really was gorgeous. "I swear! We only met a few days ago. He was just being nice when he invited me, because I embarrassingly let it slip that I have no friends or relatives here. Is he always so nice?"

Jillian smirked. "Trying to change the subject, I see…" Damn, she was good. I had been. "But I'll bite. Yes, actually, my brother is probably one of the nicest, calmest people you will ever meet. He's truly one of the best people I know."

The love in her voice when she spoke about him made my chest hurt. What that must feel like, to have a sibling you'd do anything for…

Then she sighed. "However, you do not want to see him pissed off. That man, as calm and collected as he may be…whew, there is another side there when he gets crossed. We've always called it 'when the Wolf comes out.'"

She saw my confusion and waved her hand. "Oh, not over anything trivial or silly. He lets most things roll off his back. But if someone messes with the people he loves…it's not good. I mean, it's the reason he stepped down from being, like, a lead detective to being an old beat cop. Isn't that what they called them back in the day?"

I nodded. "Yeah, I think so." He *had* been a detective! "So, wait…what happened?"

I adjusted in my seat to look more directly at her, and she did the same, scooching in closer to me. I tried not to look too interested, but oh, was I ever. We were like two conspiratorial little girls whispering gossip.

She lowered her voice and said, "I probably shouldn't be telling you this, but Wolfgang beat the living shit out of another officer he worked with. I mean, we are talking within inches of his life. Like three other guys had to haul Wolf off the guy."

I was about to ask why he'd beaten the guy up so badly when footsteps sounded down the hallway and Wolf appeared in the room. Jillian and I both looked up over our shoulders and smiled at him at the same time.

"Finally! We were wondering where you were," Jillian said. "Took you long enough."

Wolf glared at us, two mugs in one hand and one in the other. "What were you guys talking about?"

I cleared my throat. "Oh, nothing…just about how maybe I might have picked the wrong creamed corn." I grabbed my hair tie off my wrist and tied my hair into a low ponytail, trying to act natural.

"See? She did like mine better! We just didn't want to hurt your feelings." Jillian pouted at her brother.

"Uh-huh, sure. I'll go ahead and pretend that's what you were talking about." He brought over the mugs and sat in the brown leather chair across from us.

"Thanks, bro," Jillian said.

"Yeah, thank you. This smells excellent. I haven't had hot chocolate in forever." I blew into my mug and took a small sip, letting the creamy goodness and bite of Baileys warm my throat. It was so yummy. I closed my eyes, slowly licking the marshmallow fluff off my lips and savoring the flavor. When I opened them, Wolf's heated eyes were on me, his mug unmoving in front of his mouth. He seemed to come back to himself and looked down, took a sip, and lowered the mug into his lap. "Good, huh?" he choked out.

"It's perfect." I told him and kept my eyes on him until he met mine again.

It was quiet for a moment, and then Jillian spoke up. "Well, you should taste mine. It's even better," she quipped with a twinkle in her eye. "Alright you two, I'm going to head up to bed and crash. Be good." Then with a wink at me, Jillian left the room.

Chapter Fourteen

We sat there in our separate seats, quietly sipping our hot chocolate and looking at the fire. I held the mug close to my mouth, letting the steam moisten my skin. It felt so nice. Not just the hot chocolate or the fire, but being here. Being with people who cared for one another. Being here with Wolf.

"What are you thinking about?" Wolf's smooth voice brought me out of my head.

"Oh, nothing. Just that I like your family. They all seem like really great people. I'm glad you brought me."

He got up, set his mug on the coffee table, and moved toward the empty spot next to me. I lifted the blanket for him to sit down. His body instantly warmed my right side as he draped his left arm along the back of the couch behind me and slid his right hand under the blanket onto my thigh and gave it a light squeeze. "I'm glad you came. I really wanted you to be here." I opened my mouth to speak, but he cut in, "And no, I don't think of you as some charity case. I mean it, Raven—I'm glad you decided to come with me."

His hand started to make slow circles on my thigh. My skirt slowly moved up, up, up. His breath hitched as he reached the top of my leggings and realized they were only thigh-highs.

I leaned into his shoulder, still clutching the mug. I knew my breathing had started to increase as my body reacted to his touch. A tingly warmth pulsed down deep. His fingertips toyed with the lacy tops of my tights, and I knew. I knew I wouldn't stop this. I couldn't stop this. Didn't want to stop this. That one-and-done idea I'd had— how stupid of me.

His fingers moved toward my center, and his hand spread my thighs apart ever so gently. With one finger, he slid my underwear to the side, and I couldn't help but imagine what if I had been wearing some other panties, like the ones Salone had grabbed me. Thank God I had bought these cheap, lacy undies.

His lips found my neck as his fingers played. They did all the things—slow circles, small tapping, and slight pulling. I'd been wet from the moment he touched my thigh, and I was almost embarrassed by it. His touch was tantalizing, and I couldn't stop myself from slowly moving into it. I wanted more. I wanted it all. I wanted him.

I moved then, and his hand pulled back. I set the mug down on the coffee table. Without having to say anything, our bodies moved into place. He lay on the couch, and I straddled his thighs as I undid his pants. He lifted himself to pull them down farther as I moved up. He was hard and ready. I hadn't thought I could get any wetter, but I did.

His hand slid up my skirt to ensure my underwear was still off to the side. He rubbed me softly for a moment, moving my wetness around.

"Fuck," he moaned.

"Yes, please," I said, smirking down at him. He looked up at me with a smile and then stopped rubbing me. He grabbed either side of my hips and slid me slowly onto him. He was so big. I mean, I knew that obviously, but he just felt amazing. Even better than the other night, somehow.

After a few slow, tentative movements of him lifting me up and down, he asked, "You good?" I nodded and leaned down to kiss him.

We kissed while moving slowly like that until he reached up and pulled my hair free from its band. My hair cascaded down around us.

"You're so beautiful," he said, his eyes burning into me.

"Right back at ya." I leaned back up. I started to move faster, the couch squeaking with each movement, so I slowed.

"Don't stop. No one will hear, and if they do, trust me, they won't investigate. Just don't stop," he groaned.

So, I didn't. What did I really care if they heard us? It wasn't like I was going to see these people ever again. I did keep my moaning to a minimum, though. I have *some* class, but I rode Wolf, his hands digging into my hips, mine on his biceps, until we both found our bliss, me finding mine a moment before him as if my coming was what he was waiting on. Always so thoughtful.

I moved off him and shifted my underwear back to its proper place. He slid his pants back up, but didn't button them. He scooted to the edge of the couch to let me squeeze between him and the back of it, then he lifted the blanket over both of us. We lay there quietly with my head on his chest. He had been looking at me the entire time, which was unlike the first time we had hooked up, when it had been almost pitch dark. I felt a little self-conscious, but he had said I was beautiful.

I smiled to myself and let the bliss settle in. That had just felt...incredibly good. His breathing was steady, and I realized he was asleep. I closed my eyes, allowing myself to feel safe and happy. This wouldn't last forever, but there was no reason I couldn't enjoy it for just a little while.

A little while came and went before my eyes popped open, and I gasped. I sat up, leaning one hand on Wolf's chest to prop me up and put my other hand over my mouth looking down at him.

He sprung up. "What's wrong? Are you okay?"

"We didn't use a condom!" That's why it had felt so fucking good. Damn it! Damn it! All the wine, his famous hot chocolate, his fucking tantalizing fingers, and my need for his...well...all of him, I'd completely blanked!

"Are you not on birth control?" He was blinking his sleep away.

"No! I haven't fucked anyone in years, and the pill messes with my hormones! Why do you think I asked you to wear one the other night?"

Our voices were intense but too quiet to wake anyone. "For STDs. I don't know!" He was clearly as rattled as I was. His golden hair was mussed, and even though I was in panic mode, I still found myself thinking he looked endearing.

I pushed myself up and moved over him to stand, and he slid into a sitting position and rubbed his eyes and head. "It's okay. I mean, do you know what time of the month you're at for your cycle?"

My cheeks heated slightly. Oh my God. I wasn't going to discuss my period with this dude… but he did have a valid point. I took a deep breath and thought for a moment. I was going to start my period probably in four or so days. I sat down next to him. "I think—I think we are good. I should be out of that window."

He put his hand on my back and rubbed it slowly. "Alright, see? It's okay. I know we don't know each other extremely well, but I swear to you, I don't have any STDs. So, you're good on that front, too."

I took another deep breath. Obviously, I cared about not getting an STD, but getting pregnant was something that just couldn't happen. There was no way I could be a mom right now; it would be a disaster.

"And," he continued, "if you want to play it even safer, I can pick you up the Plan B stuff from the pharmacy. Completely up to you." He was treading lightly, not knowing my thoughts on abortion. *Smart guy.*

"No. I'm fine. I'm positive I'm out of that window. Sorry, I just freaked out a little. I should have thought of that before waking you. I'm sorry," I said again.

"Are you kidding? Don't be sorry. It was stupid of me. I just didn't use a condom for so many years because Tiffany was on the pill. It's just not something I think of, which is dumb."

"So what's with the condoms in your bedside table?" The question was out of my mouth before I could stop it. When he didn't answer right away I tried to quickly rebound and waved my hand, "I don't know why I asked that. It's seriously none of my business."

He grabbed my hand in his. "No, it's fine. I was hooking up with someone from work. It was a 'friends with benefits' trial run that didn't pan out well."

"Oh," was all I could muster…so awkward; but he continued.

"Yeah, things sort of got uncomfortable with her every time she saw me talking with any of the other women we worked with. I mean, we're talking she was jealous of even Salone, who's 62 and married to one of my good friends, Emily. So I had to tell her we were better off as just friends."

Damn, poor girl. She had clearly wanted to be more than just friends, and I sure couldn't blame her for that.

After we took a few moments to catch our breath, we decided to head to bed. I didn't want to know what he'd said to his family for them to not think it weird he was sleeping in the same room as his supposed "friend" he'd just met. There was a cot in the corner of the bedroom with a pillow and blankets, but they had to know we were at least hooking up. Clearly, Jillian had put it together, and the glance Lauren had thrown him earlier in the kitchen—aw, who was I kidding? They all knew, probably even little Sara.

Wolf had gone to the kitchen to put our mugs away and I cleaned myself up in the bathroom, brushing my hair and teeth. I tried my best to be quiet so as to not wake Sara and Jillian in the next room. After I changed out of my Thanksgiving attire—thankful now that I had accidentally gotten the thigh-highs—I slid under the covers while Wolf took his turn in the bathroom.

As I lay there, I suddenly realized there wasn't a top sheet on the bed. He must have removed it earlier in the day. My heart swelled in appreciation. But this felt too normal; it wasn't right. I should have felt awkward and out of place with this cop and his family in his childhood home, but I didn't. Jesus, I'd just killed someone only days before, and there I was playing house with this guy. What the fuck was wrong with me? This was definitely a problem. A problem I would think about the next day, though. There was never any sense in trying to solve problems late at night or after multiple glasses of alcohol.

Now, since I was wide awake, I thought about what Jillian had spoken of earlier. Wolf had been a lead detective for the Green Bay Police Department. That was huge!

When Wolf slipped under the comforter next to me, shirtless and in his boxer briefs, he immediately pulled me to him. I rested my head on his chest as I had the last few nights, with his arms gently around me, and I slowly stroked the curve of his muscled chest.

"So, Jillian mentioned you used to be a lead detective, but you chose to step down. Why is that?"

His hand, which had been playing with my hair, paused for a moment and then resumed. "Of course, she did. I knew you guys had been talking about something much more interesting than corn." His voice held a note of amusement. "Do you want the short, simple answer or the long, dramatic one?"

"Do you have to ask? Drama, obviously!" I lightly smacked his chest.

He sighed. "Alright then. First off, I wasn't a lead detective. That's not even a position, but I *was* in the Investigations Division and had been for many years when I found out Tiffany was cheating on me with a guy I worked with."

I couldn't help myself; I sat up and looked at him. "*What? She* cheated on *you*?"

He adjusted and sat up against the headboard. I moved then to sit cross-legged and faced him, grabbing the throw blanket from the edge of the bed and wrapping it around me before he continued.

"Yeah, I came home for lunch one day because she'd been sick. I was going to make her some soup. When I got there, she was sleeping on the couch and her phone kept going off with texts. I went to silence her phone so it wouldn't wake her when I saw the message. She must've been pretty drugged up with meds because she didn't wake up the entire time I scrolled through her texts with him." He laughed to himself. "I didn't even say anything to her. I just let her keep sleeping and went back to the station."

"His name is Jason Brickson, and I'll never forget seeing him at his desk that day when I walked back into work. He actually looked up at me and smiled. He was about to say hi, I think, when I punched him right in the face." Wolf looked a little uncomfortable then, and his hands were gripping the comforter. "I sort of blacked out after that. But later, I saw the surveillance footage. Three other guys had to pull me off him. I almost killed him. I didn't mean to do that. I didn't mean to almost kill the guy. Hurt him a little, obviously." He shook his head. "Outside of the affair, he's truthfully a decent guy. We were friends, and he'd been coming over to our house for years to watch football—dinners and game nights, ya know? The betrayal part of it all was too much, and I guess I just lost it. I couldn't and wouldn't take my anger out on Tiffany physically, so I did it to him. He ended up spending a few weeks in the hospital and had to have multiple surgeries, two of which were on his face."

I watched Wolf but didn't say anything. I just grabbed his hand in mine. I could feel the guilt of what he had done to Jason permeating off him.

He continued, "Jason never pressed charges, and everyone at the station just acted like nothing had happened. I knew all of them were on my side, but what I'd done to him was not right. I went in the next day and asked to be put on patrol. I thought maybe if I worked a less hectic schedule, Tiffany and I could work through things."

Oh my God, this sweet man still wanted to save his marriage after all of that! "What position were you in the Investigations Division?" I asked the question gently. He had seemed like he wanted to be vague about it for some reason.

"Captain."

I knew it! I knew he wasn't just a regular cop. With those diplomas and his overall demeanor and awareness, this guy was clearly an irreplaceable asset to the city of Green Bay.

"So you were Detective O'Dell's boss?"

"Technically, his boss's boss, but yeah," he said carefully.

It made sense then, why he'd been able to let the detective know he was in talks with me. He may be a patrol cop by position, but he still held some authority amongst the detectives regardless of his current status.

I nodded. "So, you working less hours…did it not help with Tiffany?"

"When she found out what I'd done to Jason, she lost it. She screamed at me and said she wanted a divorce. Said I was a monster and she loved him. She filed for divorce the next day and had my shit packed up for me. The department gave me administrative leave for a couple months, so I stayed here with my dad and then eventually bought my house a few months ago."

"Does Jason still work there?" I asked, imagining how awkward that would be if he did.

He chuckled. "No, he quit. He's healed up now, a lot less of a pretty boy than he used to be, but healed. I've heard he's working for the BCSO." I knew that meant the Brown County Sheriff's Office. "Last I heard, he and Tiffany were engaged. They'd apparently been together for a couple years already by the time I finally found out. Stupid, I know. I was clearly an idiot." He shook his head as if he couldn't believe it still.

"No, you weren't." I reached out and placed my hand on his beautiful face looking into his clear blue eyes. "She's the idiot. Honestly, she must be the dumbest person on this planet to throw away a relationship with you. You are the kindest person I think I've ever met. She didn't deserve you." And I believed that. But I was saying too much. Too much of how I felt.

I was drunk, and he'd been incredible with me downstairs after my condom freak out, but I really, truly believed everything I was saying.

He smiled, and his hand moved up to my hair. He ran his fingers through it. "It's funny, but I haven't missed her. Everyone thinks I'm probably sad or heartbroken, but I'm not. The betrayal is what affected me, not the divorce. Part of me realizes now that we'd been growing apart for years and things should have ended a lot sooner. What she did was wrong, of course, but her falling out of love with me and in love with someone else wasn't wrong, and I can't fault her for that. Not really. Not when I'd fallen out of love with her long before. I just had been too busy to notice."

Add *understanding* to this dude's resume and strike off *cheater*. He was great. Just great.

Perfect, even.

He pulled me down into the bed to get comfortable again. "Seriously, don't feel bad for me. I don't. Not anymore, and especially not right now." He stroked my back and kissed my forehead. I melted into his touch and closed my eyes, dreamily aware of the sound of the side lamp being clicked off.

Chapter Fifteen

I woke to sounds from the bathroom and a light humming tune coming from inside—sweet Sara getting up for the morning. Wolf's arms were around me, my back to him. This was the first morning I'd found us in a spooning position. I must have turned away from him at some point in the night only for him to find me again. My hair was tucked up and his face was buried into my neck. I knew he had woken, too, when I felt light kisses on the back of my neck and shoulder. I shouldn't have liked it, but I did. Damn it, I really did.

I liked waking up in his arms, and I liked that he was kissing me first thing in the morning, and that was a big problem, because that was not what I'd been planning on. I'd planned on a quiet, simple life. I hadn't planned it, actually; I had decided it. It had been a heavy decision, too. I know I'd broken hearts that night a little over a year ago when I'd left the reservation in the middle of the night. But I'd decided it had to be that way. I was done with relationships of all kinds. I was done with people I cared about dying. How could one person handle so much death? I knew I couldn't handle losing one more person I cared about, and so, the loner lifestyle had been my choice. Now...now I wasn't so sure about it, and that was the problem. Self-doubt is the one thing that can turn your mind, your heart, and your soul into a roiling mess of angst, and now here I was, percolating in it.

Hooking up was one thing, but meeting family and getting sweet kisses in the morning were entirely different. I turned in his arms, sweeping my hair back behind me. I was aware that my head pounded slightly; too much alcohol the night before, way too much. My breath was probably horrible, so I lifted the blanket to cover the bottom part of my face. "Good morning."

His hand stroked my back, under my shirt, as his arm stayed around me. "Good morning." He smiled at me sleepily.

A light knock came at the door. "Uncle Wolf? You up?" Devon's voice sounded through the door.

Wolf arched his neck up a little. "Hey, bud. Yeah, I'll be out in just a minute." When footsteps could be heard walking away, Wolf continued his back rub. "Sorry, Day After Thanksgiving tradition we started a few years ago…we go on a morning run."

I groaned. "A run? It's probably thirty-five degrees out and— you're not hungover?"

He sat up, releasing me, his chiseled body begging me to run my fingers down it. I resisted the urge partly because I knew my head would pound harder if I moved.

"Not really. Are you?"

"Yeah. My head hurts a little. I'll be fine, though."

He leaned down and kissed my forehead gently and then multiple light kisses flitted across my head. I should've stopped it, but it was sweet, so I closed my eyes, accepting the gesture. To my surprise, it actually seemed to help my head for a moment.

After he had used the bathroom and changed into his running clothes he came back over to me in the bed sitting on the edge. He pulled me to him and caressed my cheek softly with one hand. "Take your time resting."

"Actually, I think I'll take a shower." That would hopefully help me feel better.

"Towels are under the left sink. I'll be back in an hour or so." With one final kiss on my forehead he left the room, softly closing the door.

I slowly sat up, slowly walked into the bathroom, and slowly took a shower, alternating the hot and cold water on my head to ease the pain. I managed to wash my body where it mattered the most but didn't bother shampooing my hair.

My head was still pounding when I walked back into the room with a towel wrapped around my body and another one on my head. Waiting for me on the nightstand was a mug of steaming coffee, a glass of water, toast with butter, and two pills.

I sighed in relief and sort of felt a little like crying. It had been so long since anyone had taken care of me like that.

I ate the toast quickly to avoid taking the medicine on an empty stomach, downed the water next after the pills, and then leaned back in the bed with the coffee.

Sounds of the others waking up and moving about the house were new to me but somehow comforting, the creaking of this house unlike mine and, therefore, not triggering. I drank the coffee quietly, enjoying the dim light of the early morning streaming in through the windows. After a while, I set the mug on the nightstand, scooted down on the bed, lay my head on the pillow, and closed my eyes.

The shower turning on in the bathroom woke me, and I found that the throw blanket had been draped over me. I looked at the clock and saw it was 8:30 a.m. I had slept for over an hour, and it had done me well; that and the food, water, coffee, and meds Wolf had left me. I sat up and took my hair out of the towel which was still wrapped around my head. I finger-brushed my hair out and then braided it into one long braid. I got dressed quickly in jeans and a soft knitted cream sweater and headed out of the bedroom with my plate and cups.

I didn't want to be in a space with a bed and a naked Wolf. Okay, not the truth; I *did* want to be in a space with a bed and a naked Wolf. In fact, I wanted to slip right into that shower with him and have him fuck me quick and hard, but I had let things go further than they ever should have. A simple "make me forget fuck" had somehow turned into more. If I knew that, then he had to know that, and what was going through his head, I didn't even want to know.

I walked out the door and almost slammed right into Jillian. "Oh, hey, Raven! Sleep well?" She fluttered her eyelashes at me in an exaggerated attempt to look like a know-it-all.

I laughed. "Yes. This home is very inviting and comfortable. Slept like a baby." We walked down the stairs together and the smells of syrup and bacon were overwhelmingly intoxicating as we headed into the kitchen.

Jim smiled at us and kissed Jillian on the head as she came over to him for a hug. "Perfect timing, girls. I just pulled some more German pancakes out of the oven."

Sara looked up from her plate at the table and ran to me. "Oh, Raven, I love your hair! Maybe after breakfast, you can braid my hair like that, and then I can paint your nails?"

I grinned down at her. "Sounds like a great plan!"

Lauren smiled from where she, Devon, and Drew were enjoying their own breakfasts. "Yes, a great plan, sweetie. Come back and finish eating, and let Raven eat, too."

Devon, still in his running gear, had a heaping plate of food.

Jillian grabbed my half-drank coffee mug from me. "You want more?" she asked.

"Yes, please."

Jim handed his own mug to his daughter and said, "Warm up, please, sweetie."

She moved to the coffee pot and filled up the mugs. "Sugar? Creamer?" she asked me.

"Creamer, please."

She handed Jim his and me mine as I thanked her before she made herself a cup. Jim brought over more of the German pancakes to the dining room table, and we all sat and scooped up food. I had probably put on at least 10 pounds since Sunday. Ever since coming to stay with Wolf, I had eaten better and more than I had in—well, since living with Mama Elena.

Wolf came down the stairs, his eyes bright and his hair still a little damp. It curled slightly, shadowing his blond hair with dark gold. My stomach flipped at the sight of him, and I almost regretted my decision to not join him in the shower. He poured coffee from the pot into a mug before coming to sit next to me and filled up his plate.

"How was your run?" I asked.

"It was great! Cold, but refreshing. We did six miles, and Devon kept up with me the entire time."

Drew spoke then. "I've been trying to convince him to ditch football for cross country like his dad, but apparently 'cross-country dudes don't get girls.'"

Drew used air quotes for the last part, and Devon's cheeks were pink as he confirmed, "No, they do not."

Wolf looked at Drew. "Tell us, Drew…how many girls did you date during high school?"

Drew gave a cocky laugh. "I'll have you know I dated plenty of girls, aaaand I was prom king. So yes, cross-country and track-and-field dudes do get girls."

Devon quietly mumbled, "Yeah, in the 1900s maybe…" Everyone laughed at that. Even Drew.

"Touché, son. Touché."

After breakfast, Sara and I prepared for our hair-and-nail appointment. She, conveniently, never went anywhere without her nail polish and makeup kit. She chose a deep red with sparkles for me.

We sat in the big, beautiful living room/game room adjacent to the dining area. I asked if she wanted me to braid her hair into two pigtails, but she insisted on it looking just like mine so we could be twins. Her hair had a curl that was like her mom's and not like mine or her dad's, but she didn't seem to mind the frizz which puffed around her head and told me she would just use hairspray.

"Are you Uncle Wolf's girlfriend?" she asked while she was painting my nails. She had turned her favorite show, *Spirit Rangers,* on in the background, and we were sitting on the ground in front of the TV with a slew of newspaper, nail polish, nail polish remover, cotton balls, and Q-tips. Jillian was up on one of the armchairs, her legs delicately kicked over one of the arms, reading a book. Her nails were perfectly manicured. Sara must've already known her auntie went to a nail salon because she didn't ask her to join our little party.

Jillian snorted at Sara's question, and we made eye contact and smirks over my shoulder.

I debated what to say. She was only 8 years old, but what if Wolf and I hadn't been as quiet the night before as I thought? Was me saying we were "just friends" sending the wrong message to a young girl when she knew we had stayed in the same room together? Not that there was anything wrong with me hooking up with whoever I damn well pleased, but still, she was young.

"No. Your uncle and I are just friends."

She pondered for a moment as she dabbed my finger with a Q-tip dipped in nail polish remover, cleaning up her overspill. "Do you want to be his girlfriend?"

Although the question was innocent from the mouth of a child, it was a question that I myself hadn't had the guts to dwell on. I laughed a little uncomfortably, knowing Jillian and anyone else nearby was listening. The sounds in the kitchen had died down suddenly, where the rest of the Hill family and Jim had been putting together a 1000-piece puzzle of Lambeau Field. I knew Wolf was still upstairs by the distant sounds and deep, muffled voice coming from up there. He'd gone up after breakfast with a call from O'Dell.

"I think I am really lucky to just be friends with your uncle right now. How about that?" I said and gave her a smile.

Her mouth pursed sideways. "Well, I guess that's fine. As long as you stay friends forever and come to every holiday!"

Before I could crush the little girls hopes—or lie—Jillian swung her legs off the arm of the chair and sat up straight. "Once your nails dry, Raven, I'd love for you to braid my hair as well, please."

"Ooh, yes! Then we'll be triplets! Or, or the Three Amigas, or the Three Musketeers!" Sara squealed, completely forgetting the previous conversation.

"Absolutely!" I smiled up at Jillian with grateful eyes.

Jillian's hair, to no surprise, was as silky, shimmery, and soft as it looked. It was as perfect as the rest of her. I braided it with more ease than I braided my own and was done in seconds.

"Ooh, do it again, please! That felt so good. I need go to the salon soon just for a shampoo. Doesn't it feel so good when someone else washes your hair?"

"Mmm hmm." I knew what she meant. It did feel amazing when someone else washed your hair. I took the braid out and started over.

"Aunt Jilly is going to fall asleep," Sara whispered to me as I continued to braid and unbraid Jillian's golden locks.

I had not done anything like this in years. Possibly a drunken girls' night with some friends in college, but even then, those had been so rare since I was always with Rocky. It was entirely possible it hadn't been since with Lilly in high school that I'd played with hair and nails. I looked to Sara. "This is fun, Sara. Thanks for planning it."

"You're welcome!" she beamed.

Wolf appeared in the doorway, finally done with his call.

"Hate to break this up but we have to get going," he was smiling at the scene in front of him but I sensed something had changed in his demeanor. That phone call had been a long one. Something had happened.

"No! Go away, Wolf! You're ruining our spa day," Jillian groaned. She truly was sounding as if she was about to fall asleep. I peeked around to find her eyes were closed. I finished up her braid officially and helped her up from her sitting position.

"Don't we look like triplets, Uncle Wolf?"

He smirked. "It's uncanny!"

"What's that mean?" Sara asked, confused.

"It means we are the most gorgeous triplets that ever graced this world, dear Sara," Jillian said dramatically and then squeezed my hand and Sara's in hers. "Thank you, Raven. I'll have perfect waves tomorrow when I take this out."

"No problem!" I said. I didn't doubt she'd have anything less than perfect if she wanted it.

Wolf and I gathered our stuff up and gave our goodbyes. Jillian, of course, broke the ice with the hugging, and after that, I easily hugged the rest of the Rivers/Hill crew goodbye.

We left with two bags full of leftovers in addition to the food containers and bags we had brought. It had only been one day and one night with these people, but I didn't want to leave them. It was an odd feeling I quietly pondered for a while as Wolf drove until I realized Wolf was just as quiet. He, too, was pondering something. That call.

I broke the silence. "Was that call about my case? Is there something you don't want to tell me?"

He sighed and then responded, "Something may have come up."

My heart pounded quickly. Did they figure out I had lied in my account of what had happened that night? Did they know I had intentionally shot Caleb in the dick? My mind started racing as I forced myself to ask, "What has come up, exactly?"

Wolf glanced at me, taking his eyes off the road for a moment. "I don't want to freak you out, and I probably shouldn't even be telling you this, but I think you should know..." He trailed off, clearly having an internal battle with himself over telling me or not.

I was freaked now. "What is it, Wolf?"

He sighed again. "We've been in dealings with the assailant's family, and let's just say, things got a little weird. This family is not normal, Raven. Like, they are really fucked up from what we are learning. A huge group of creepy, backwoods type for lack of better words."

I felt a small relief at knowing it wasn't about the gunshots but also a little confused. "Are they wanting to press charges or something?"

He was quiet, then answered, "Uh…no. They didn't really say as much."

"What does that mean? Like this is all going to go away? Maybe they knew he was a shit person and are relieved in a way he's gone?"

Wolf's face was one of concern as he drove down the highway. "The officer who spoke with his mom and brothers said the whole vibe there was wrong. He said multiple people were walking around the house, and the looks they gave him were almost…in his words, 'hungry.' He called in for backup because he was so creeped out by just standing in their living room that he wanted someone to be there with him. Another officer showed up and felt the same off vibe, so they quickly apologized for the family's loss and asked if there was anything they needed. It was a brother who apparently said the words, 'We'll take care of it ourselves,' and then shut the door on them."

Yes, very weird, especially when two police officers were creeped out by this family.

Was it a threat? Were they threatening me?

"Obviously, he hailed from a fucked-up group, it would make sense his family was that type. I mean, he had to come from somewhere. So, are you thinking they want to—what, avenge their piece-of-shit brother or something?"

"We don't know that, but I told O'Dell we need to keep our eyes on them. I'm going to talk with him more about it tomorrow. I'm not in that department anymore, so it's not my job to do any sort of follow-up work for your case, but I'm going to see what I can find out."

Why had he told me this? Now I had to worry about an entire family that possibly wanted to eat me alive. Perhaps literally.

"Okay, well, great. Juuuust great." I squeezed my hands together to try to relieve the urge to scream.

"Look, I know you're probably going to go back to your house soon. If you want to stay longer at my house you can, or I can stay with you at yours for a few days. I know you can take care of yourself, and I'm not trying to insinuate that you can't. I just know you haven't wanted to be alone, and if you're not comfortable yet, I don't mind being there."

I thought about it. I hadn't wanted to be alone, and I still didn't want to be alone, especially in my own home. And if I was being completely honest, the thought of going back there alone after what I had just heard was a little terrifying. But was getting too close to Wolf even more terrifying? Yes, at this point it was. Plus, he said he, "didn't mind," which sounded like he probably did mind but was being nice. He was probably over having me staying at his house and wanted his alone time back. Here I was, wanting, craving to not be alone, and I was sure he probably couldn't wait to get his house back to himself.

"You've been more than accommodating and helpful, Wolf. Seriously, it'll be good for me to rip the Band-Aid off."

He just nodded as if he understood and kept driving.

Chapter Sixteen

When we arrived back at Wolf's, all talk of when I'd be going home disappeared because he received a call from BluePearl. Rosie was ready to go home.

I left in a hurry to go get her as Wolf told me he would get things set up. I wasn't sure what that meant, but I didn't care; I was going to get my baby back.

At the vet, one of the technicians helped position a big crate in my car and carry Rosie into it. They told me I could return the crate at a later time. She had been so excited to see me they decided to up her dose of medications to calm her. Rosie was the sweetest, most well-behaved dog I had ever met. In fact, her attacking Caleb Conners the other night was the first I had ever seen any ounce of aggression toward a human. I knew she had sensed his evil.

When I pulled up to the house, Wolf came out immediately to help carry her in. When he set her down inside, her tail wagging, she sniffed him and determined we were safe. I stopped short, spotting exactly what Rosie saw. A dog bed that was sitting in Wolf's living room. She walked slowly over to it, sniffing it and the contents next to it, stuffed animals and chew toys.

Then Wolf reached into a box of treats, and she gladly accepted a few. There was no sense of unease from her toward him at all. I would now and forevermore trust her judgement.

A bowl of water and another of food were set on the floor in his kitchen. I leaned down to pet her while she sniffed the new bed and toys. "Did you just buy all this?"

He rubbed the back of his neck. "Yeah. I wanted her to be comfortable here. I didn't want to only set out a blanket for her."

My heart swelled, and it was a moment before I was able to get any words out. "I…I can pay you back for all of this." I motioned with my hand toward the bed and bowls.

"No, don't worry about it. I wanted to do it for her. She's a hero."

He was right. She was a hero. "Thank you. We really appreciate it." I stood up, feeling so many different emotions, but mostly I was just grateful. Rosie was happily lying in the bed now, tearing into a honeybee stuffed animal.

Wolf was too good to be true. He was an angel sent to us. I didn't deserve him, and with my track record, I figured I should probably get as far away from him as possible.

"Are you okay?" he asked, trying to catch my eyes with his own.

I had been trying to force them back, but tears came streaming down my cheeks. Wolf came up next to me, and I turned into his chest. His arms surrounded me. "I'm overwhelmed…with everything—your kindness, and that Rosie is going to be okay. I thought she was dead, and she's going to be okay!"

He held me tight. "I'm sorry if I've overwhelmed you, but not sorry I've been kind," he said, and I laughed, leaning back to look at him.

"It's not your fault I'm overwhelmed. I've been alone for so long. I forgot what it was like to have people be caring and understanding. I'm just really grateful is all. I know this nightmare is almost over and we will go back to our lives, but I want you to know how thankful I am for you. You didn't have to do any of this these past few days, yet you did. I know I'm not a charity case to you, but it wasn't your fault any of this happened to me, and you let me interrupt your life, and for that, I am just overwhelmed with gratitude." He pulled me back into a hug and I let him, enjoying his strong arms and the feeling of safety.

The evening centered around Rosie. Ensuring she was comfortable, she ate, that she didn't jump or run, and that she was given her meds. Wolf actually ordered pizza and salads for delivery and shocked me by eating three slices of the meat-lover's pizza. I had never seen him eat so unhealthily. It was clear he didn't want to leave Rosie's side for very long either. When it was time to go to bed, Wolf carried Rosie and the dog bed into the room without me even having to say anything. He knew there was no way I was going to let her out of my sight.

When we got into his bed, he grabbed my hand in his. "I go back on shift tomorrow, but if I hear any news about the investigation, I will let you know as soon as I get back. You know, you really need a phone."

I ignored the phone comment. "When do you think you'll be off work?"

"I should be done around five, and then Devon has a basketball game at seven. I was thinking about going if you wanted to join."

A high school sporting event could be fun. I hadn't been to any live sporting event since Rocky and I had gone to an amateur hockey game five years earlier.

"Maybe. I'd love to watch him play, but I want to make sure Rosie is comfortable here first. I'll see how she does tomorrow. And—" I took a breath, knowing my next words needed to be said "—as much as I appreciate everything you've done for us, I think it's time we go back home. Maybe the day after tomorrow, if that's okay with you?"

He held my gaze, rubbing his thumb along the back of my hand. "Of course. I'm good with whatever you want to do."

He's just being nice.

I knew it was time to go.

We'd both passed out quickly, in each other's arms of course, but without any sexual advances. I woke up very early to Rosie's wet nose against my arm. I quietly grabbed Wolf's coat out of the closet and slid into some of his boots to take Rosie outside. We took it slow down the one small step from the front door stoop to the front lawn, and she did great, even with it being 30 degrees out. She, unlike me, had never seemed to mind the freezing weather here after moving from California.

Once we came back in from the cold, we settled back in our respective beds. Wolf had turned over onto his stomach away from the side I had been on. The warmth and comfort from his arms not around me had my mind racing. I wanted to go to him. I wanted to put my arms around him. The urge to do so had me hating a part of me.

I knew if I allowed myself to pursue that physical touch, it would be crossing a line. The sex and the cuddling when he initiated it was different. I hadn't yet been the one to initiate the cuddles and spooning. He was always the one to reach for me each night when we first got into bed. So, I pushed the want and desire down and away and turned to face his bathroom door. After contemplating for far too long about how I was going to get out of the pickle I had put myself in with Wolf, I found sleep again.

I woke later to the smell of coffee on the nightstand, but Wolf had already left for work. Rosie had a toy in her bed, and she was happily shredding it to pieces. The coffee was still hot, and a note next to it read that he had given Rosie her meds already. I moved out of his room to the front window to see his truck going down the street. I had just missed him.

It was better that way.

After a quick breakfast of fruit and nuts, I spent the rest of the day catching up on work and tending to Rosie, ensuring she stayed calm. Fortunately, she was out of her puppy stage at now almost four years old, so keeping her calm was relatively easy. I answered emails and went through recent orders. Things were in a really good place, but I needed to get back to my home office soon, where I had my printer and mailing supplies, or I was going to get some bad reviews and have to issue refunds, which was a pain in the ass. I also tried to mentally prepare myself for going home the next day.

I had hoped Wolf would come back for lunch, but after about 1:00 p.m., I helped myself to some of the leftover food from Thanksgiving, of which there was still so much.

Finally, around 5:30 pm, I heard the door to the garage open. Wolf came in holding his keys and a plastic bag. I was curled up with a book from his collection, Rosie on the ground next to the couch. She tenderly but excitedly got up and moved toward him as he entered, her tail wagging.

"Hi, Rosie! Sweet girl." He quickly went to the kitchen and grabbed a treat for her. "How was today?" he asked as he patted her head. He looked up at me with a sparkle in his eye. "She looks happy."

I placed the book down on the arm of the couch. "Yeah, she seems really good. She's been taking it easy, which is great. I was able to catch up on some work, but it's good I'll be going home tomorrow. I need to get to my home office for some order preparations. Any update on the investigation?"

He smiled at me as he took off his coat and gear. "Yes. The investigation is now closed."

I stood up quickly. "So, that's it? It's over? No charges from the Conners? No court?" Rosie, sensing my excitement, came over to me.

"There will be no charges pressed. We haven't heard a peep from the Conners. The conclusion of the investigation was, as you already know, self-defense. It's over."

I sighed with relief.

Wolf set down his wallet, keys, and gear on the counter. He went to the fridge, took out two beers, and cracked them open, handing me one. We clinked the bottles together, neither of us sure what to exactly say about such a weird cheers, and then took a sip. I sat back down on his couch in a daze. It had only been a week, but it had felt like a lifetime of panic and worry. Now, it was over.

He sat down next to me. "I know I have to work tomorrow, but if you don't mind, I'd like to meet you at your place when you head back home if timing permits. Salone will likely be with me, though. Would that be okay?"

I nodded, unsure of what to say. I was happy but also not.

"I also got you something."

My heart started thumping a little quicker. *He got me something...*

He walked over to the bag he'd brought in and took out a phone. "Look, before you say anything, it's nothing fancy, and I had the person disable the apps and internet and stuff. It has my number in it, Salone's, and the station's. In case you need to get ahold of us for any reason."

I took it from his outstretched hands. "Is this because of the Conners?"

He looked uncomfortable and took another swig of his beer. "Yes and no. I did get to do some digging into them today, and something is definitely off about that family, but mostly, I just wanted you to be able to get ahold of me if you feel like being alone is too much. I'm sorry if I'm overstepping."

I shook my head. "No. You're right. It's good to have, in case of emergencies. Thank you. This was thoughtful." I looked at the phone and then smiled at him.

"So, do you think Rosie will be okay here alone for a bit? Want to go watch some high school basketball?" He waved his eyebrows up and down and I laughed. Getting out of the house did sound like a good idea, if just to take my mind off what would surely be an intense morning.

"I think if we put her bed in the crate from the vet, she'll do just fine," I told him.

As Wolf showered, I made us turkey sandwiches with the leftover turkey meat and rolls and heated up some of the other leftovers, making up a dish of what I recalled seeing him eat, and then one for me. The only thing he hadn't had was Drew's rolls, but I was going to give it a shot anyway. I knew he wasn't big on carbs, but he had indulged in the pizza the night before. I sprinkled salt and pepper on top of the turkey and replaced the top of the roll and set the table. I added a glass of water behind both our plates. Since I wasn't sure who was going to drive to the game, and we had each just drank a beer, I didn't think it was smart to open another one. I mean, he was a cop.

When he came out, he was dressed in jeans and a blue sweater which made his eyes even brighter. He stopped short and stared at the table.

"I know, I know, but Drew's rolls are seriously incredible, and I barely put any mayonnaise on yours."

He didn't say anything for a moment, and I thought maybe I had fucked up more than I realized preparing—if you'd even call heating up food preparing—a meal in his kitchen. He did say he was a kitchen snob…but then again, I'd helped myself to food in his kitchen a couple of times, so that couldn't be it.

He came over and sat down in front of his plate. "My mom always used to make leftover turkey sandwiches with the rolls for us the days after Thanksgiving. I had forgotten about that until now." He grabbed the sandwich, and as he took a bite, he closed his eyes. "This is really great. Thank you," he said.

My heart cracked a little.

Chapter Seventeen

I washed the dishes and cleaned the kitchen while Wolf took Rosie outside for a bit and then got her set up inside the crate. The fact that he slipped her some treats and toys made it worth it for her. The medication she was on from the vet made her drowsy, and I knew she'd be sleeping soon. It made me feel a little less guilty for leaving her, but not much. Luckily, the game was in De Pere, which was less than 15 minutes from Wolf's place.

When we got to Devon's basketball game, the smell of the gymnasium and popcorn had my mind going back in time to memories long forgotten. Memories of friends and laughter and cheering. Of Lilly. It almost took my breath away.

Wolf led me into the gym after paying our way in, and I followed him up the stairs to where his family was sitting. Jim, Jillian, Lauren, Drew, and Sara were all there.

"Raven!" Sara exclaimed. Everyone seemed surprised to see me, and little Sara was beyond excited, smiling and bouncing in her seat.

I didn't know why I hadn't thought of it, but I was surprised to see them as well. Of course, they would be there to cheer on Devon; that's what families were supposed to do.

After saying our hellos and getting a huge hug from Jillian, I found my seat next to Sara. Wolf sat on the other side of her, next to Lauren. Lauren leaned in and whispered something in Wolf's ear. He shook his head as if to say, *Not now!* and nudged her with his shoulder. I wondered what that was about.

The game was intense, and Devon was not just good, he was by far their best player. Wolf really got into it, and I realized had probably been just as good when he'd played, because he seemed to understand the sport on a higher level than I did. But no one was more into it than Lauren. She was jumping and moving with every pass and shot, cheering louder than anyone in that gym. A part of me felt bad for Devon, who had to be embarrassed, but I hoped he knew he was lucky to have such a supportive mom. I sometimes wondered, had I grown up with my mom—really either of my moms—how their supportiveness would have shown through. Would it have been the calm, quiet sort like Lilly's mom had been or the loud, in-your-face kind like Lauren? Either would have been just fine with me.

Drew and Jim were much calmer than Lauren, but when a rough foul had Devon hitting the ground hard, both men jumped to their feet. Devon, of course, was fine, but Drew was muttering about a flagrant foul, and Jim was jeering at the ref to do his job. Sara and I giggled together at all the excitement around us.

"Can I tell you a secret?" Sara asked me during a time-out.

"Absolutely. What is it?"

"Well, I'm not like my family. I actually don't like playing sports. I don't want to play basketball or run track."

I could relate. I had never played any sports except for the forced softball during P.E. classes in middle school and floor hockey in grade school.

I glanced at Lauren, who could clearly overhear the conversation, then said, "Hey, that's okay, but it's always healthy to stay active. Is there another activity you think you might want to try someday?"

Sara thought for a while. "I do like watching the cheerleaders and all the fun cheers they get to do! They get to have pretty outfits, too. I think that would be fun!"

"Didn't you know, cheerleading is a sport not just an activity?"

"Really?" she said, shocked.

"Oh yes! They have competitions and do really intricate cheer routines. It's a very cool sport!"

And then before I knew it, I was telling her about Lilly, who had been the captain of the cheer team when I was in school, and that I thought Sara would be an excellent cheerleader, and, if she worked hard, maybe even make captain someday. Lauren, overhearing the conversation, smiled at me with grateful eyes.

At half-time, Jillian took Sara to get some snacks at the concession stand, and I scooted closer to Wolf as Lauren leaned over him and squeezed my hand thoughtfully.

"Thank you for that! She's been feeling really guilty lately that she hasn't joined any sports teams like her brother, even though we told her as long as she's doing some type of extra-curricular, we are happy. Though she's doing musical theater, she still feels bad about not playing a sport. She knows both her father and I were college athletes. And, sure, I guess we've always assumed both our kids would be interested in the same sports we were. I never thought about cheerleading, but that seems right up her alley!"

Wolf nodded in agreement.

"Did your friend go on to cheer in college or professionally?" Lauren asked, very interested. She was clearly a competitor. I could see her already imagining herself rooting for Sara years down the road at some college game she was cheering at.

"Lilly? Oh, no. She passed away when we were sixteen." I couldn't keep the sadness out of my voice.

"Oh, Raven. I am so sorry!" Lauren exclaimed. Her soft hand, still clasping mine, gripped a little tighter with a caring squeeze.

I could feel Wolf's body tense next to me. One more piece of my sad life clicking into place for him.

"I was lucky I was able to experience her friendship as long as I did. Every moment with Lilly was beyond special." Even as the words escaped me, I didn't want to go there. I really couldn't open the door regarding Lilly. At least not in a public place. Thankfully,

Sara and Jillian returned at that moment, and Lauren pulled her hand away as Sara squeezed in between Wolf and me.

Sara, Jillian, and I shared popcorn and licorice the rest of the game. It was a blow out! Devon's team ended up winning by thirty points, and Devon was the leading scorer.

After the game, Jim gave his goodbyes and headed home while Lauren, Drew, and Sara also gave us their farewells, then went to wait for Devon to get out of the locker room.

In the parking lot of the school, Jillian turned to me and Wolf. "I'm hungry! Let's go to Delilah's!"

I had wanted to get straight back to Rosie, but figured we had a little time before she woke up or needed to go out, so Wolf and I met Jillian at the diner back in Green Bay.

Delilah's, apparently, was a diner the Rivers family had grown up going to and often still enjoyed. It was your classic diner, and I presumed, just by the looks of everyone comfortably sitting and chatting throughout, that most were regulars getting their evening slice of pie or cup of coffee. But just like when I'd been at the store the other day, I had an odd sense of being watched.

I glanced around the diner, taking it all in, and caught the eye of a beautiful woman further down, who looked away quickly. Odd, but I didn't dwell on it because Jillian pulled me along to a booth all the while explaining why this place was her favorite, claiming they had the best milkshakes and fries.

Having not eaten dinner yet, Jillian ordered a full meal with a chocolate shake, and I ordered strawberry. Wolf and I sat next to each other on one side of the booth while Jillian sat opposite us. The conversation flowed, and I was able to divert most of the personal questions that Jillian asked about my life by getting her to talk about her work. I could tell she knew I was deflecting, but she kindly answered all my questions with passion and vigor. If she hadn't made her career in piano, I betted she could have been a Broadway actress.

Her dramatics as she talked, always for comic relief, were a breath of fresh air.

I could sense Wolf's disappointment that any information regarding myself didn't come to fruition with my diversions. I didn't want these people to know about my sad, depressing past. It was bad enough I'd drunkenly opened up the other night about my time in foster care with Mama Elena, and then about Lilly at the game. Wolf already knew enough of the basics of my life and losses; he didn't need to know anything further.

When the food came, Jillian excused herself to the restroom to wash up. In the booth, side by side next to Wolf, I couldn't help but want to lean into him. To feel his warmth against me.

"I still can't believe your sister is sch an incredible pianist. How did she even decide that was what she wanted to do?"

Wolf grabbed my strawberry milkshake and took a quick sip before answering.

"Indulging tonight, are we?" I laughed.

"Just a sip." He winked. "Honestly, my mom's death had an impact on all of our career choices."

"How so?" I asked taking a sip of the milkshake. It was delicious! So creamy and thick. The flavor was on point, too.

"I mean, for me, it's pretty obvious. I wanted to go into the police force to help protect people and understand how criminal minds work. After her death and how she died, there was no other career choice I ever even considered. My mom had been an elementary schoolteacher, so Lauren followed right in her footsteps."

"And Jillian? Piano?" I questioned, interested in hearing the answer.

"Like I mentioned before, all of us had piano lessons. It was something my mom enrolled us in when we were in the fourth grade. She wanted us to be old enough to sit still and really listen to the teacher. Well, Jillian had been begging to start earlier than that. It's all she talked about for at least a year. My mom had already paid in advance for the lessons for Jillian before she died. It was meant to be Jillian's big Christmas present that year."

"Oh my God," was all I could say, and I put my hand on his thigh. His big hand came down over mine. This time, he trapped it there.

"Yeah, Jillian was only eight years old when my mom passed. I think begging for piano lessons was one of the main things she remembers about my mom. I sometimes wonder if my mom hadn't died, what careers we all would have chosen. If we would've ended up going down the same paths or something entirely different."

"I know what you would have done."

His eyes brightened at me, the blue shimmering from the light above our booth. "You do?"

"Yes. You would've been a chef." Wolf's eyes grew big, and he looked a little caught off guard. It surprised me that he'd never thought of it himself. He was about to say something, but Jillian slid dramatically back into the booth.

I could've kept my hand where it was, and he could've kept his there, too, but we both moved our hands apart from each other in a natural way.

"Lord, they really need to get another stall in the women's restroom here. It's seriously ridiculous. I finally just went into the men's." She shrugged.

I nodded my understanding at her—the woman who was a pianist mainly out of sheer determination and sentiment.

Just as we were finishing up, the beautiful woman I had made eye contact with earlier walked toward us, looking directly at me. Did I know her? She looked sort of familiar, but I was certain I'd never met her before. She seemed a little taller than me, probably five-foot-six, with shorter, stylish brown hair and honey-brown eyes. Her makeup was impeccable, and she was pregnant; *very* pregnant. She stopped directly in front of our booth.

Wolf looked up still smiling from something funny Jillian had just said, then his expression faltered. "Tiffany."

Tiffany? Oh, shit! I wasn't looking at Jillian, but I heard her making a sound resembling a snarl.

"Hi, Wolfgang. Hi, Jill," Tiffany greeted. She didn't even acknowledge me, which I found interesting since she had been staring me down the whole way over.

"Wow, Tif, you're like, super fucking pregnant," Jillian stated bluntly—and not kindly.

Tiffany rested her hands on her belly and rubbed slightly. "Yes, well, that's why I came over here. I was going to call you when I found out—" she was looking at Wolf now "—but Jason didn't want me to, and, honestly, I couldn't stomach looking at you."

She couldn't stomach looking at him? That bitch! I wanted to shout it in her face. The booth under me adjusted slightly, and I glanced down to see Wolf clenching it with his hand. He hadn't said a word yet other than her name. I turned back toward Tiffany, back toward her protruding belly.

"Anyway," she continued, "it's time you know so you can be prepared. Obviously, there is a chance this baby is yours. I'll call you if the paternity test for Jason is negative and we'll go from there." She took that moment to acknowledge me with a smug smirk. "Oh, hi! I don't think we've met before. I'm Wolfgang's ex-wife, Tiffany." Before I could say anything, Jillian was out of the booth and grabbing Tiffany's hand, pulling her away.

"How exciting this must all be for you, Tiffany. Can I talk with you really quick?" Tiffany looked a little perturbed and glanced back at Wolf over her shoulder. I, too, glanced at Wolf, his face one of astonishment. She smirked at me once more before being pulled along by Jillian.

Wolf cleared his throat to finally talk, but I got up and out of the booth as quickly as I could. "Um, I need to go to the bathroom."

He reached for my hand, but I stepped back. "Raven, she's full of shit. She—"

"No, Wolf, she's full of a baby, and I really do have to go to the bathroom." I walked the opposite way from where Jillian had pulled Tiffany, to where I assumed the bathrooms would be. My dumb eyes were betraying me, stinging with unshed tears. I had to get away from Wolf and that whole baby-mama drama.

The bathroom was on the other side of the diner, but the way the restaurant was set up was almost like a horseshoe with a space available for diners to come from either side to the bathrooms. As I turned the corner to go in, I heard voices clear on the other side, still in the dining area, and I paused.

"You're hurting my hand, Jill!"

"Oh, am I? I'd be hurting your fucking face if you weren't pregnant, you lying bitch. What the fuck was that?"

Tiffany made a scoffing sound. "I don't know what you're talking about."

"Give me a break! You and I both know that baby isn't Wolf's. You just pulled that shit because you saw he was happy and with someone better than you."

"That isn't true." I heard Tiffany's voice shaking and assumed she was crying.

"Oh, save it! I'll have you know I have never seen my brother laugh or smile the way he does with that girl over there. And guess what, Tiffany? They are just friends. And if some day they are more than friends, which I hope they will be—God, I hope, because she's amazing and good and he deserves that more than anything—you better not pull this shit again! How you made him feel doesn't even compare to how she makes him feel. *You* don't even compare. You saw that and are smart enough to know it, but too dumb to stay away."

I heard sniffling and then Tiffany say, "You're being cruel. Jillian, I lost in this whole thing, too, you know? I didn't just lose my marriage; I lost all of you. People I love! You think I don't think about Devon and Sara all the time? How I wish I could have gone to Devon's basketball game tonight?"

Jillian's voice raised slightly. "No. No! Don't you dare, Tiffany! Losing people happens when you don't have a choice. You had a choice, and you should have thought about the consequences of your actions before you started cheating on my brother for years. God, Tiffany! *Years!* I want you to hear something, and listen closely to me now." There was a pause and then, "Stop fucking crying, because it's not working on me. Look at me." Another pause, and then Jillian said, "Get this through your head. Do not come near my family again. Do not come near Wolf again. That girl over there, if you ever see her, don't fucking come near her. If by some bizarre chance that baby is Wolf's…then, and only then, can you come knocking on our door. You hear me?"

There was no response, but Tiffany must have made some indication she understood because Jillian said, "Good talk. Have a good night. Oh, and congratulations on the babe. I'm sure Jason will be a great father. Don't raise a cheater now, ya hear?"

I figured Tiffany's first move would be to head into the bathroom, so I quickly went back the way I'd come and headed to the booth where Wolf was paying the bill. He looked up as I sat down and turned toward me. He looked exhausted.

"Raven, that baby is not mine. With the timing…look, I just know there's no way. She's being vindictive and throwing low blows for no reason other than she saw you sitting next to me."

I knew that now, but instead I said, "Wolf, you don't owe me an explanation. All of that was none of my business. Like I said, I just needed to use the restroom."

Jillian returned with a smile and slid back into her seat. Wolf stared at his sister for a while. "You good?" he asked her.

"Never better, brother." She picked up her chocolate milkshake and slurped the rest of it loudly through the straw.

Wolf sighed. "We should call it a night."

He wasn't wrong. I hadn't wanted to crawl in bed and pull the covers over my head and cry like that in a long time.

I had felt so childish sitting there, while Tiffany had looked like a woman standing all beautiful and pregnant, her baby bump level with my head. I felt small and young compared to her. I felt stupid. That's what I felt. Just stupid. And the reality that I was feeling that way was even more frustrating.

I had started to develop feelings for this man. I couldn't lie to myself any longer because that baby bump staring me straight in the face had struck up such a fear, that I had wanted to run away and cry.

Had I subconsciously concocted some scenario in which we'd end up together? Had I really, after all I'd been through, allowed hopes and dreams to seep in through the wall I had built up? This whole time, from the moment I set down the gun and he wrapped his arms around me to block out the sight of the man I had killed to now, had holes started to form in that poorly constructed wall of mine? And the small realization he might have a baby and get back to his perfect life with his perfect-looking wife…had that really been what I feared?

Those questions flew through my head as we said goodbye to Jillian. She gave me three hugs, and as Wolf and I walked the opposite way to my car, I looked over my shoulder and saw Jillian flipping off a distraught-looking Tiffany through the diner window.

I hadn't pegged the pianist as a gangster, but I did now.

Did Wolf know his little sister had his back like that? I think he did.

Chapter Eighteen

Back at Wolf's, after a quiet and awkward drive, I told him one of us should sleep on the couch or in the guest room, thinking it would be a good way to ease me into being alone at my house the next morning.

He stood in the doorway of his room. "Raven, I swear that baby is not mine. I won't sleep in here if you really don't want me to, but I just can't help but think after what happened with Tiffany, you're trying to push me away."

Push him away? He was talking as if he knew I had real feelings for him. I sat down on the floor next to Rosie, petting her. She looked back and forth between us as we talked. "Not the case at all. Like I said, that whole baby-mama drama is so none of my business, and I don't have a thought on the matter either way."

He looked at me for a while, clearly not buying it and then sighed. "Okay. Sleep well." He grabbed his pillow and started walking out of the room.

I couldn't help myself. "You didn't even say anything. She was standing right there, saying her baby could be yours, and you just stared." It was an accusation. I wasn't really asking a question, and yet I had asked a question.

Wolf turned in the doorway. Rosie's tail began wagging as if he was coming back in.

"I know. I was not expecting to see her and especially not in that state. I panicked. I was doing the math in my head because I knew we hadn't been having sex a few months before we got divorced. So, I was trying to remember the month we actually got divorced and, yeah…" his voice trailed off.

I felt bad then. We barely knew each other, and here I was, making this man feel like he owed me an explanation. He didn't. It was absolutely ridiculous that I was acting this way because of some crush.

"Sorry. Again, it's none of my business." I turned my head away from him and looked down at Rosie. Her head angled up at me, her big eyes asking me what was wrong.

When I didn't say anything more, Wolf left the room.

I quickly got ready in the bathroom and slid into bed. It felt lonely and cold, and I did not find sleep for many hours. My mind was racing—not just about what had happened at the diner, and not just about my feelings for Wolf, but about the Conners, and Caleb, the man I had killed, and the house I had to go back to.

Not surprisingly, I had a nightmare that night. In it, I shot Caleb Conners three times, but when I walked over to look at him, it wasn't Caleb but beautiful Tiffany on the ground. I heard crying, and I turned to find Caleb sitting on my bed holding a baby. A knife lay next to him as he rocked the baby in his arms, shushing the baby like a comforting father would.

I screamed and lurched up in bed. Wolf came running in the room as Rosie barked and came over to me. Wolf's arms wrapped around me, and I curled into him, shaking. His hand stroked my hair, and he wiped my tears as they flowed.

"I've got you. You're safe. It's all going to be okay," he said, over and over.

I clung to him. Hoping and wishing he was right. I'd be okay.

When I woke up again hours later, he was lying next to me on top of the covers. My hand was in his, and my heart hurt at the sight. I had grabbed Rocky's hand that fateful morning to hold it. It had been ice-cold and felt wrong, and I knew, I knew he'd been gone a while at that point, but I still tried to wake him up. I still begged and pleaded for him to be okay.

Wolf's hand was warm and tight encircling mine. He wasn't dead. He wasn't Rocky. He wasn't any of the nightmares in my life that had happened previously.

Maybe he was a second chance. A second chance at happiness and love and life. *Life.* That was the point, wasn't it? The point of the wall I had built and the solitude I had strived for. Not just the simple fact that it hurt when those I cared for died, but that they *died.* All of them. My birth mom, my adoptive parents, my best friend, my foster mom, my boyfriend—they all died, and the common denominator was that I had loved them. What if I was cursed and me spending time with Wolf or his family meant something bad would happen to them? Was I a Grim Reaper of sorts, and I didn't know it? The thought thoroughly creeped me out. And if I was the Grim Reaper and I kept up whatever this was with Wolf, did that mean he'd die?

And there it was. The real reason I'd run that night from the reservation and had been keeping to myself ever since. I was afraid that if I let myself care about someone, they would die. Was it crazy? Yes, probably. Was it rational? Maybe not, but at the same time, maybe it was, with what I had been through.

I'd gone to the reservation a year earlier not expecting to actually meet any relatives of mine but rather learn some of my roots—learn why I looked the way I did. Since I hadn't grown up with any religion or spirituality, I'd thought maybe I would find that there. What I had found was an entire family on my birth mother's side who had all been missing me every day since the state had come in and taken me from them. What I'd found was a loving, amazing family who gave me and Rosie instant love and security.

I spent almost two weeks with them—my grandparents, uncle, and aunties, and then, right when I thought *this is it, this is where I belong,* my grandfather had a heart attack and was rushed to the hospital. The entire family was torn up because he was by all accounts a healthy man and that sort of thing had never happened before. When we got word that he was in stable condition, I waited until everyone was asleep, and Rosie and I hightailed it out of there to Green Bay. I couldn't help but think I had brought my curse with me, that I was the reason my grandfather had almost died. If I left, then they would all be fine. They'd be safer away from me. Whether or not I was being completely ridiculous, I still didn't know.

One thing I knew for sure was this was it. This had to be it. This time with Wolf, it was ending today. The investigation was over. I wasn't going to be charged with anything, and I was going back to my house. So, what would it hurt if I let myself have him one more time? Just one more time, to let myself feel good and happy and not alone. I could pretend just once in these early morning hours that I wasn't me, I was someone else who didn't have baggage. Someone who had had a happy life. Someone who hadn't just shot and killed someone a week ago. I could pretend I was someone worthy of Wolf. And I'd pretend that Wolf…well, he'd still be Wolf. God, he'd still be him. But I'd pretend this perfect, kind, beautiful, thoughtful man was mine, and he wanted me as much as I wanted him.

I didn't doubt there was an attraction on his side; that had been made evident a few times. But I wasn't naive enough to think he had developed true feelings for me. How could he? I hadn't given him a lot of opportunities to get to know me—I mean, really know me.

He hadn't even mentioned dating me after all of this. He'd only dragged me around to spend time with his family because he was too nice to leave me alone.

None of that mattered, though. All that mattered was I could pretend.

I turned toward him and kissed his forehead softly, both his cheeks, and his closed eyes. He groaned and let go of my hand, moving his to my lower back and turning his body to me. Although it was dark, I could see his eyes were now open.

He didn't say anything, and I didn't either while he returned the kisses to my face. Soft, sweet, slow kisses on my face and neck and down to my breasts as he lifted my shirt up, pushed the covers away, and moved his body to be above me. I ran my hands down the muscles of his bare, smooth back. God, he really was perfect.

His kisses lowered to under my breasts, and his hands moved down my arms as he kept his body lifted. His kisses then trailed slowly down my abdomen, and he tugged my sweatpants and underwear off, tossing them to the end of the bed as he continued his kissing and now sucking, getting closer inch by inch to my wet center.

I would normally stop this, but I was pretending. Pretending we cared for one another, and if we did, then I would let this very intimate act happen. And so, I didn't fight him and didn't nudge him back or away like I had the first night he'd attempted this. His mouth found its target so softly, so incredibly slowly. His kissing down there was…it was everything.

My body was arching up, but I couldn't stop it. I wanted more and faster, but he didn't give me that yet. He gave me tender, slow licks and sucks. His mouth did what his fingers had done the other night, and I was in ecstasy. When he moved his tongue out of me, he kissed me slowly up until he parted me again and sucked on my most sensitive part. I curved up and into his mouth, and he pushed my hips back to the bed, firmly pinning me down as he inserted two fingers into me. It didn't take long for me to lose all control as he sucked while his fingers moved. I screamed in release as my body shuddered against him.

Once my tremors slowed, he released himself from my lower half and trailed kisses back up my body. I lifted my shirt completely off me as he removed his underwear, and then my hand found him, hard and smooth. There were no words from him this morning. No dirty talk. Just manly moans and grumbles that made me almost come again. I tightened my thighs against his hips, hoping he could sense my desperation for him to be closer to me, to be inside me.

He continued his kisses up to my chest. His mouth moved to suck on my nipples, causing me to squirm with anticipation of what was to come. As he moved up to kiss my lips, he simultaneously reached toward the nightstand and opened the drawer. I put my hand on his arm. "It's okay. I'm going to start soon, remember?" He didn't respond, just placed his hand to the side of my face, and caressed softly.

We could just make out each other in the early autumn light streaming through the windows. He kissed me then as he eased into me. Our bodies moving languidly, sweetly. I'd have thought we were making love instead of fucking, but I knew that couldn't be the case because we barely knew each other, but damn it, I could pretend.

He flipped us over, so effortlessly with his strong muscles, moving me on top. I continued the slow rise and fall motion. His hands moved up and down my back, sides, and ass, and then with one trail down his hands dug in, and he released himself into me. He was gripping my ass and his throbbing inside me had me coming with him. I hadn't expected that; I hadn't thought I could feel this way with him. It was bliss.

I leaned down, my hair flowing over us, and I kissed his neck before my lips found his again. We kissed, him still inside me for a while longer, until he grabbed me to him fully and moved us to our sides. I turned, and he curled his large body behind me, and he found sleep again, fast. I didn't waste the time I had left with him in these final moments by leaving to use the restroom like I normally would, to clean myself up. Instead, I fell asleep, still pretending.

When I awoke, Wolf was gone. A cup of coffee on the nightstand was cold. The crash of realization that my time with him was up was nearly debilitating. I had to go back to my real life now—the one that didn't consist of Wolf or friends or a loving, inviting family.

I lay in his bed for as long as I could, until I heard a *ding* coming from the phone Wolf had bought me. I moved toward it and saw that there was a message.

Wolf: Good morning, Sleepy Head. Salone and I can meet you and Rosie at 11:30 a.m. Will that work?"

It was 9:00 a.m. now. I responded we would be there. Damn it, I had a phone now. I sat up, and after taking care of my own bathroom needs, I took Rosie out. After we both had our breakfast and she had her medication, I found cleaning supplies and set about cleaning his entire bathroom. I had used it for a week, and it was the least I could do.

After, I took a quick shower. My body sore in all the right places, had me washing myself carefully, trying not to think of what had happened just a few hours ago.

Once out of the shower, I swept my hair up into a messy bun and got dressed. I packed up all the things I had in his bathroom and bedroom and put them in a couple plastic grocery bags I found in his pantry. I didn't want to use his duffle bag again and then have to figure out the logistics of getting it back to him. This would make it easier to cut the cord. I gathered up the things for Rosie and moved everything by the front door.

While Rosie lingered in the dog bed, I thoroughly cleaned his kitchen, then moved on to dusting all surfaces, vacuuming, and mopping the entire house. I could never repay him for his kindness, not really, but I could clean his place.

Once I was done, I loaded up the car, with Rosie last. She pressed her nose against the window, seeming a little hesitant to leave, and I looked back at her. "I know, girl. I feel the same way." She let out a sigh and put her head down on the seat.

Chapter Nineteen

After a short stop to drop the crate off at the vet, I pulled up to my house to see Salone and Wolf standing out front. I got Rosie out and walked toward them. Rosie moved straight to Wolf, her tail wagging.

Salone reached down to pet her. "Here is the hero! Such a good, good girl. Yes, you are! Yes, you are!"

Rosie's tail wagged even more.

I hadn't expected such a tough old lady like Officer Salone to do puppy talk. I knew, had Rosie felt her normal self, she would have jumped up on Salone in a heartbeat.

Salone looked at me. "Hi, Raven. I hope you don't mind. Officer Rivers explained this was the first time you'd be back to your home. How have you been?" She smiled, still petting Rosie.

So, he hadn't told anyone that I'd stayed with him, not even his partner. "Oh, yeah, no problem. I've been holding up," I said, avoiding looking at Wolf.

"I know you've been in contact with Officer Rivers here a few times, and I just wanted to let you know how happy I am that it seems you'll be able to move past this whole mess. If you ever need anything, please don't hesitate to call us. Officer Rivers said he gave you my number, as well as his and the department's?"

"Yes. Thank you, and I appreciate it. I'm ready to try and get back to my normal life." Again, I made sure to not look at Wolf while I said that last part. I didn't think I could handle what I might see in those crystal-clear blue eyes.

"Would you like us to go in with you?" Wolf asked.

I did, but I didn't. For some reason, this was the first time I *did* want to be alone since the whole ordeal began. Maybe it was because the other officer was present and so clearly knew nothing about Wolf's and my little arrangement. I wasn't sure if we could keep things seeming professional if I had a breakdown.

"No. I think I'm good. Thank you, Officer Rivers and Officer Salone. For everything." I hoped Wolf knew that last part was meant for him.

Wolf hesitated as if he was going to insist they go in with me, but he finally said, "Of course. Like Officer Salone said, please don't hesitate to contact us about anything."

I stared at him, my eyes moving to his mouth—the mouth that only hours before had been on me in the most intimate of ways. I forced myself to smile. "Thank you. Come on, Rosie. Let's get you inside." I moved toward the door as Salone started walking away.

"Do you need any help bringing stuff in?" Wolf asked, still standing on the sidewalk.

"No, I've got it." I looked back at him, and he nodded.

"Okay, then."

"Okay," I said back and waved.

But he still didn't move. I heard Salone say to him, "She said she's got it, man. Let's go."

Once they were finally out of my line of sight, I opened my door and led Rosie inside. The house smelled clean. Very clean. I brought Rosie to her dog bed in the living room and forced myself to walk to my bedroom. Rosie's claws clicked on the hardwood floors as she followed me instead of lying down. My heart was pounding, and my hands were shaking, but I had to do it. A cold sweat broke along the back of my neck. I was sure I was standing right where Caleb Conners had stood when I'd heard the floorboards creaking. I pushed the door open, and Rosie barked and growled but stayed next to me. It seemed she, too, was going to have PTSD from this incident, and, of course, that would have made sense. She had been the one physically hurt, as well as mentally, and I couldn't protect her from that.

I walked in to find it clean, too. No dead man lying on the ground. The flooring was visibly a shade lighter where the blood had been, likely from whatever cleaning detergent they had used. I would need to put a rug there or something. I took deep breaths, grabbed my pillow off the bed, and Rosie and I exited the room, shutting the door behind us.

I walked around my house, ensuring everything was how I had left it. In my kitchen, that large cast iron pan was still on the stove, the unwashed knife I'd used to slice tomatoes still on the cutting board. I'd left it that evening to clean later. Later ended up being a week later, longer at this point, as I was in no mood to do more cleaning after doing it all morning. Especially not a heavy-ass pan. I felt physically drained, even though I had only been awake a short time.

I went into my office and threw the pillow onto the couch I had in there. This was where I would sleep now. For how long, I didn't know, but I couldn't stomach sleeping in my bedroom, and the living room felt too open, too exposed.

I went about printing and labeling mailings while Rosie slumbered next to me, getting lost in my work for a few hours. I told myself that keeping busy would ease me back into normalcy.

I placed an order pick-up for groceries and other essentials. I raised a brow when I noticed all the foods I had selected were basically whole foods. Wolf's healthy eating habits had rubbed off on me, so I threw in an order of strawberry ice cream just to void the fact he was having an ongoing effect on my life. He was gone now. I had to go back to what life had been before him.

I grabbed the phone he got me and checked it. No messages, no calls. I didn't want him to call or message anyway; that would be dumb.

I flung the phone to the end of the couch and got busy with work again.

Chapter Twenty

Later that evening, I returned home from dropping off shipments at the post office and picking up my grocery order. I set the multiple grocery bags slung through my arms down just inside the door, keeping the door ajar so I could quickly take Rosie out before unloading it all.

"Sorry, Rose, that took longer than I thought." I turned to the kennel I had put her in, but it was open, and she wasn't there. Had she gotten out somehow? I was sure I had locked it.

I was about to call her name when pain lanced through my back and I was thrust forward, my neck cracking as my torso jerked before my head and neck knew what was happening. I fell face-first to the floor, my nose just barely missing the ground as my hands found their way in time to brace myself.

My front door slammed shut, and I heard the lock click.

I scrambled up onto my feet as quickly as I could and looked up. A man, slightly bigger than me, was standing by my door. He had scraggly, long brown hair that hit his shoulders; it had a wet sheen to it. Had he already been in my house waiting until I entered? Or had he slipped in when I set the groceries down? It didn't matter, only one thing did. "Where's my dog?" I demanded as I placed a hand to my back. Fuck, it hurt.

"I don't know what you're talking about." His voice was eerily familiar, rough and evil sounding. "You don't have a dog. So, I can't tell you nothing about no dog or where it is."

Holy shit, holy shit, *holy shit*! He did something to Rosie! I couldn't handle her getting hurt again. "Where is my dog, you piece of shit?" I yelled.

He smiled at that. "Long gone by now. That bitch is long gone. Just like you're going to be."

Déjà vu, I was having déjà vu. This couldn't be happening. He pulled a gun out from behind his back, and I realized this *was* happening.

"I want to know something," he said as he inched toward me as I inched backward, sliding around my kitchen island. "When you killed my brother, you worthless cunt, did he say anything before he died?"

My chest was heaving in uneven breaths. Caleb's brother. The Conners.

Their threat had been real.

But I couldn't help myself, "I don't know what you're talking about. You don't have a brother. So, I can't tell you nothing about no brother or what he said." It was stupid, to give him a taste of his own medicine and use his own words back at him, but I was so angry, so fucking angry that this was happening again.

He may have sounded dumb when he had spoken earlier, but it wasn't lost on him that I was being condescending. His face contorted into a terrifying grimace, and he cocked the gun and aimed it at me. "That's not how this is going to work. *I'm* in charge here! You do what I ask when I ask it, and you answer my fucking questions truthfully!"

His voice increased into a shout, and he strode forward. "We've been watching you, Raven Lowe. You and your cop boyfriend."

My breathing hitched at the mention of Wolf. The knowledge that these people had been watching me for possibly days made my stomach drop, and I slowly raised my hands up, forcing my voice into a calm, kind tone. "Look, all your brother said to me was that he was going to kill me—that's it. He broke into my house to kill me and I…I shot him. It was self-defense."

"So, you had to shoot him three times? No, no, what I think is that you wanted to kill him. I think you liked shooting him, so you did it two more times! He probably begged you to let him go. You'd made your point and stopped him from hurting you. You didn't need to shoot him again. I think you're an evil little slut who needs to be taught a lesson."

I had been slowly backing up as he had been advancing, and I bumped loudly into the counter next to my oven. My hands went behind me as if I was trying to brace myself. There was nowhere for me to go; the door to my right was just a shallow pantry with a glass door. I had to move quickly, but he had that gun. I needed to distract him.

"No, not true. It was dark in the room, and I knew he had a knife, but I didn't know where he was, so I just shot a few times, but I didn't mean to kill him. I had never shot a gun before." That last part was true.

He was close to me now, an arm's length away. His right arm extended with the gun in his hand aimed directly at my face. "Really? Guns are so fascinating. You know, it's funny, I had always told Caleb to carry a gun. In fact, I gave him this one for his birthday last year. But no, he always said he preferred the knife. That it made less noise, and he liked to slice." I realized then these brothers had been very close, and there was no way I was going to talk this guy out of killing me for the death of his brother, who he clearly loved.

He was looking at the gun now and seemed zoned into a memory. I took it as the only moment I would have. The knife I'd managed to grab off my counter when I purposefully backed up to it had already cut me. I'd maneuvered the hilt down into my non-dominate left hand. It was slippery with my blood, but I knew I had one chance to get this right.

I clenched the knife hilt as hard as I could and whipped my hand out, my left hand moving up and then down fast.

I'd sliced his right arm.

He screamed and dropped the gun, but I didn't waste a second and grabbed the large cast iron pan from behind me with both hands, my left hand thrumming in pain from the cut. With all the strength I could muster, I swung it down on him as he reached for the gun.

The sound was sickening as I heard a crunch and he went down, crumpling to the ground. His body landed on top of the gun, and it terrified me. What if he grabbed it and sprung back up and shot me? I slammed the cast iron pan down again and again, finally dropping it on the ground. It landed on his outstretched hand, and I heard another crunch.

I ran to my kitchen sink and hurled. Still sure that he was going to jump back up like in the movies, I wiped my mouth fast on my coat sleeve.

I needed to get out of there, but I had to find Rosie first. I ran through the house quickly searching for her. She was nowhere to be found. I unlocked the front door and moved out toward the sidewalk. It was dark out, and the streetlamps were on. "Rosie! Rosie! Come here, girl!" Where was she?

She had to be okay. She just had to be.

I heard a noise to my right and turned abruptly, my hair blinding me as it swung across my face. It had loosened fully from my hair tie during my frantic search for Rosie. I quickly fingered it away to see a woman, probably a few years older than me walking a small Frenchie on the sidewalk in front of my house.

"Sorry to startle you. Raven, right? I'm your neighbor, over here in the green house." She pointed to the house to the right of me. "My name is Shandra. Is everything okay? Can I help you?"

I stared at her for a moment, unsure of what to say. "I, umm…no." No, certainly things were not okay. I needed to call 911. I needed to call Wolf. The phone! I had a phone now!

I was about to go back inside, but Shandra came closer to me, stopping short when her eyes caught sight of my hand. "You're hurt."

I looked down and saw blood dripping onto the asphalt. "Let me call for help, Raven."

I nodded and then turned back toward my house, yelling for Rosie before a moment of clarity clicked, and I threw over my shoulder, "Call 911. There's another fucking dead guy in my house, and I can't find my dog. I think he did something to her, but I...I don't know."

I distantly heard Shandra on the phone giving my address as I entered back into my house. The man was still motionless on the floor, blood pooled around his head.

I walked into my office and grabbed the phone that was still laying where I had tossed it on the couch. I clicked in and saw that Wolf had messaged me a few times but I didn't read them. Instead, I just replied one word: *Conners*.

My phone rang immediately. Wolf. I answered. "Hello."

"What's going on? Are you okay?"

"No. She's gone, Wolf. Rosie is gone. I don't...I can't find her. And I had to kill him. I think he's dead. No, he's definitely dead. I heard a crunch. And I just, then...I puked. I don't know where she is. I need you to help me find her."

I knew I wasn't making sense, but none of what had just happened was making sense to me. Rosie was gone—after I had just gotten her back. How could this be happening?

"Raven, where are you?" Wolf's voice was urgent, and it sounded like he was moving around.

"I'm in my office." I had just told him I needed him to help me. Why did it matter where I was?

"Where is the man?"

"In my kitchen."

"I need you to get out of the house now. Did you call 911?"

"My neighbor did. Wolf, are you going to help me or not?"

"Yes, I'm coming over now! I'll be right there. Raven, get out—"
I hung up, feeling hollow and sick and angry. I put the phone in my pocket, and walked out of the house.

I distantly knew my hand was bleeding everywhere and my back hurt. I met Shandra on the sidewalk as sirens blared and vehicles stopped in front of my house. Other neighbors were coming out of their houses. Shandra's husband, I assumed, came out and stood by her side and picked up their frazzled dog.

Salone's face came into my view. "Raven! What happened? Paramedics! We need someone over here now! Raven? What happened?"

I looked at her, feeling numb. "He's in the kitchen. It happened again." Then she was gone, and I was ushered to the back of the ambulance.

Wolf showed up soon after. He wasn't in his uniform, which made me realize I didn't even know what time it was. I supposed he'd been talking to me, but I couldn't seem to answer. After several failed attempts to get a response from me, I heard him discussing me with the EMT. "What's wrong with her?"

"As far as I can tell, it's just a slice in her hand. She'll need stitches and, well, I don't know what else is wrong with her because she's in shock and not talking."

Wolf straightened. "Raven? Look at me, please."

I turned my gaze to his beautiful blue eyes. "She's gone, Wolf. Please help me find her."

"Of course. We'll look for her. I'll make sure everyone is looking for her. But right now, I need you to tell me if you're hurt anywhere else." His eyes were a mixture of a fierceness and concern I hadn't seen before. "Did he touch you?"

"I think he kicked me in the back. My back and neck hurt a bit, but I'm fine."

He sighed in relief. "I'll take her to the hospital to get stitched up," he said to the EMT. He helped me out of the ambulance and led me into his truck.

I sat in the passenger seat, holding my wrapped hand in my lap. I saw him speaking to Salone before getting in the driver side. "Drive slowly." I told him as he started to move. I leaned out of the window and screamed Rosie's name over and over. After a moment, he rolled his window down and did the same. I fought against the crippling thought that it might be pointless, that she was likely dead. It made me want to kill the bastard all over again, and that scared me. I hadn't wanted to kill him in the moment…had I? No. No, of course not. He'd had a gun pointed at me. I defended myself.

When we walked into the ER, my body started shaking. Wolf wrapped me in his arms as we waited to be seen and held me as I shook. He didn't ask me what had happened until we were back in the room, and they had already stitched me up. He'd known I needed time to process. Finally, while we were alone, waiting for my discharge paperwork, I told him everything—and this time, I didn't leave any details out.

"I'm so sorry Raven. I should have known that they would retaliate. I should have been there. I'm so sorry." He hung his head.

"It's not your fault, Wolf." I put my good hand on his head and stroked his hair. Then I did something I had wanted to do for some time. I told him the truth.

"I—I lied to you. To everyone." He looked up. A hint of hurt flashed in his expression, and I realized lying to him was not the right thing to admit, but I had to.

"I don't want to know," he said, utterly shocking me.

I ignored him.

"The first attack. I told the truth about everything except…I did aim that second shot exactly where it landed. I meant to hurt him there." He didn't say anything, just looked at me. "I thought he'd killed Rosie, and he was saying sick, disturbing things. I just kept thinking about the other women he had most likely hurt before, and so I aimed and shot him in the crotch. I'm sorry I lied, and I know I should probably be charged and convicted with something. Obviously, it was wrong in the eyes of the law, but I don't regret it. He was a bad person, Wolf."

Wolf was quiet for a heartbeat and then said, "I don't want you to repeat what you just told me ever again, to anyone. I forgive you for lying if that's what you need to hear, and if it helps even further, I knew your story didn't add up with that second shot."

I looked up at him. "You did?"

"Yes. Remember—many years being a detective. I surmised as much; I'm sure O'Dell did, too. It didn't matter to me how that piece of shit died, though. Just that he hadn't hurt you and he was gone. You weren't wrong in your thinking about what he had done to other women. We were able to match his DNA to six previous crimes."

I started to cry at that, and Wolf pulled me into a hug, careful of my sore back and neck. "I'm sorry this happened to you again." He said, his voice muffled by my hair.

I was, too, but more than feeling sorry, I was feeling angry that it had happened. Very angry.

"I need to find Rosie."

"Raven, there is a possibility…a high chance that she…" he trailed off.

My cheek was pressed against him as he still held me, and I cried more. "I know, and if that's the case, then I just need to find her so I can bury her. I need to do that for her." I felt him nod, and he brought a hand up to stroke my hair.

After the nurse came back in with the discharge and aftercare paperwork, we headed to the station. Salone had called on the way back and said she was waiting for us there with fresh clothes for me. If she thought it was weird Wolf had taken me to the ER instead of the ambulance, I didn't know, but I couldn't wait to see what clothes she had picked out for me this time.

I knew the blood on my clothes was from my hand, and I was ignoring the fact that there was splatter on my jeans lower down. I had to let myself believe that it belonged to me, or I would strip the clothes off me right then and there.

When we got to the station, Salone led me to a bathroom, where I changed into white joggers, a purple long-sleeved thermal shirt, and socks with little snowmen on them. At least this time Salone had grabbed me a light-green fleece jacket and my Ugg boots. I was definitely no fashion snob, happy to purchase my own clothes from Target or even secondhand stores and didn't care about brand names, but, my Lord, I couldn't fathom what this woman wore when she was off duty.

As Salone walked me back to a recorded room, she told me there had been no sign of Rosie on the premises but that my neighbors had still been out looking for her when she'd left. It made my heart hurt, knowing perfect strangers, people I hadn't even tried to get to know over the past year, were looking for her out of the kindness of their hearts. I didn't deserve it, but Rosie did.

In the room, I gave my verbal statement to Detectives O'Dell and Daniels and wrote everything out just like the last time.

As I recounted what happened again and again and again, I thought maybe my anger would start to dissipate, but it didn't. It only increased. Why had both of these men thought they could follow me, enter my home, hurt my dog, and attack me? I had a pretty good idea it had to do with the fact that I was a woman, and if that was the case, they had messed up—because I had defended myself. Somehow and someway, I had been the one to come out of the incidents, and they were the ones gone.

"What was his name, again?" I asked Salone as she and Wolf escorted me out of the station. They were going to take me back to my house to gather some of my things because I'd said I wanted to stay the night "somewhere else." I was sure Wolf and I would go to his house once we figured out how to do so discretely. What an insane, rollercoaster-of-emotions day it had turned out to be.

"Rylan Conners. One of the younger brothers of Caleb."

One of the younger brothers? Great, there were more.

"How many brothers are there?" I asked, my jaw clenched, causing my voice to sound how I felt—pissed off and scared.

Wolf looked down at me as we walked and said, "Well, there were a total of five brothers and now three remain, plus two sisters, and they have multiple cousins we are still learning about. The more we gather about this family, the more dangerous we believe them to be. And with Rylan clearly trying to take revenge for his brother's death, it's even more evident that you need to move, and then you can enroll in the DOJ's Address Confidentiality Program."

I could see the wheels in his head turning. Thinking and planning how to not let them come after me again. But I wasn't going to move. I wasn't going to hide. I was going to find my dog. But I didn't say anything about that; instead, I changed the subject.

"Can we look around the house for Rosie again after I get my things?"

Salone nodded and Wolf agreed. I knew they thought the outcome was bleak, and so did I, but I couldn't completely give up hope that I would find her.

I wouldn't. Not ever.

She was all I had.

Chapter Twenty-One

When we started to pull up to my house, Salone swore, "Damn it. How do these bastards learn about this shit so fast?"

There were multiple people and cameras outside my home.

"Neighbors, probably," Wolf muttered.

I thought about Shandra. Could it have been her? She didn't seem the type to call the media, though.

We got out of the cruiser. Wolf and Salone were on either side of me as we tried to maneuver through the small throng of people blocking my front drive. My name was being called from several directions, and before I knew it, a woman's wide face was planted in my vision, stopping me in my tracks.

"Raven! Darcy Goodwin, from the Wisconsin News, Channel 5. We've learned that within a week, two men—Caleb Conners and Rylan Conners—attacked you in your home. Brothers. Both of these men are reported to now be dead. What can you tell us?"

Salone started to shove the woman out of the way as Wolf tried to move the camera.

My blood boiled as it pulsed through my body. All I'd been trying to do was live my life, in peace, with only Rosie by my side. Now, everything had descended into chaos—strangers were trying to force me to relive my worst nightmares on television, and I didn't even know if Rosie was still alive. Air felt thick as I struggled to fill my lungs and adrenaline flooded my veins.

"What do I have to say?" I spoke loudly above the crowd, and their chatter died down, aware I was talking.

Wolf looked to me, his hand still on the camera lens as the cameraman dodged to move away from him. "Raven, don't talk to them."

I ignored him, my anger rising as my fists clenched, trying to keep an imaginary hold on the control which was quickly evaporating.

"Yes, Raven, can you shed some light on what happened?" Darcy was bundled in a puffy black coat with a fur-rimmed hood stuffed around her poorly dyed blond hair, and her makeup looked like it had been applied by an excited pre-teen girl.

My resolve snapped as the full weight of the week's events finally crashed down on me. "Well, Darcy, I'll tell you exactly what happened. Both of those *fuckers* thought they could follow me, break into *my* home, harm *my* dog, and then attack me!"

Darcy's excitement was evident. She was almost physical vibrating. "I'm so sorry that happened to you, Raven. How were you able to protect yourself?"

A cruel laugh sounded from me. My voice sounded foreign, even to my own ears. "I protected myself by any means necessary. Do you hear that, Conners family? I'm alive, and Caleb and Rylan—" I spat their names out of my mouth like the filth they were "—are dead! *Fucking dead!* So the rest of you can come the fuck at me and see where it gets you, too!"

Darcy's eyes were popping out of her head, but I couldn't stop myself, even as Salone was swearing under her breath and pulling at my arm to get me inside. Wolf and other authority members tried to get people to leave the premises, but they were just blips in the background to me.

"And for that matter—" I looked into the camera "—any piece of shit out there who thinks they can do what those two did and just break into a single female's home and do God knows what to them…you can come the fuck at me, too! I'll be here, waiting! Come and get me!"

At that point, Wolf and others had created enough distance between me and the media, enabling Salone to usher me away and into my house as further shouts of my name trailed behind. I was vaguely aware of Darcy Goodwin high-fiving her cameraman.

When I got in the house, I immediately looked into the kitchen. The body was gone, but the blood and oil were still on the floor. I walked over and stood near the island facing the kitchen sink where I could see remnants of the contents of my stomach. I heard the door shut, and a few moments later, a loud bang behind me had me jumping around, and Salone instinctively moved her hand toward her gun. We both stared at Wolf, who had just pounded his fist on my kitchen table.

He was glaring at me.

"God damn it! *God damn it,* Raven!" He pounded his closed fist again. The table moved slightly, and Salone looked as shocked as I felt. Gone was the calm, kind man I'd come to know, replaced by someone I didn't recognize. Had the Wolf come out?

"What the fuck were you thinking?"

I just stared at him, still dumbfounded by his fury.

"Why did you do that? What the hell!" He started toward me, and Salone quickly moved for me, too. His hands grabbed my upper arms. "Why the fuck did you just do that?"

Salone was trying to get in between us, her hands on Wolf's chest attempting to push him back. "Rivers! What the hell is wrong with you? Back up, man!" When he didn't budge, she looked from him, to me, and back to him. His face was seething, and he never took his eyes off me.

Realization hit her, and she took her hands off Wolf's chest, backing up slightly. "Holy shit, you guys are screwing? Shit!" She moved away from us, sitting down at the kitchen table and putting her face in her hands.

His grip on my arms wasn't painful, but it was firm, and after what I had just been through and how he'd just talked to me, I didn't fucking like it.

"I truly can't fathom what is going through your head right now for you—"

I cut him off. "No, you can't. You can't possibly fathom because it wasn't you this happened to, *again*! I had to kill someone, Wolf, *again*! Who came in to hurt me, *again*! Who hurt Rosie, *again*! And you know what? *Fuck you!* You don't get to talk to me like this! You barely know me. Get your hands off me!"

That seemed to have some effect on him because he dropped his hands instantly and had the decency to look ashamed. I turned then, walking into my office…bedroom…whatever it was.

"And whose fault is that?" he yelled after me. "You haven't exactly made it easy to get to know you. What the fuck are you so afraid of? That you'll actually make a friend? You'll actually develop real feelings?"

Yes and *yes*, but I wasn't going to warrant that with a response.

He followed me to the room and stood just outside the doorframe.

"I don't know what you thought this was—" I made sure to use past tense as I turned on him, "—but you aren't my boyfriend, you aren't my friend, and you certainly aren't the boss of me. You were just a distraction! So kindly fuck off! I can say what I want, to whom I want, and how I want!" I shouted.

His eyes seemed to shutter at that, but the next thing he said was calmer, quieter. "You may not care about your life, and you may not want to hear this, but I do. I do care about your life. I care about y—"

"Don't! Don't finish that. I don't care! I don't care what you think or feel. So don't tell me!"

I couldn't believe he was going to go there. I had seriously fucked up. I knew that now. I knew all this trying to forget and enjoying the comforts of staying with Wolf was stupid. I was stupid for letting myself get close to someone. I needed to end this before one of us really got hurt, and I didn't even mean physically. *Which, thanks to my little tirade out front, could definitely be a possibility at this point.*

He sighed and wiped his face with his hand. "Okay, fine. I won't. Here's what I will say, though. What you just did out there was not only a death wish for yourself, but it was completely and utterly irresponsible and selfish."

I gaped at him. "What the hell are you talking about?" *Selfish?* I had never thought of myself as a selfish person.

His large body curved toward me with anger, and something else bright in his eyes. "You think it was purely coincidental this guy knew the first night you'd be in your home alone? No. No! It's much more likely this psychopath had been stalking you since learning about what happened to his brother. Stalking *us*! So, do you think that maybe, just maybe, he knew where I live? Where my dad lives? Where my nephew goes to school? Hell, Raven, we are only just learning about what a warped family the Conners are. Now that two of their kin are dead by your hands, how do you know you didn't just put my family in danger with your little invite out there? Your neighbors in danger, for that matter?"

I hadn't regretted what I had said back there. I hadn't. But I did now.

Wolf was right. Rylan had been stalking me. He'd known about my "cop boyfriend" and had said "we've" been watching you. My heart started pounding.

I looked up at Wolf—and screamed in his face. *Screamed.* Like a maniac. He took a step back.

"Why couldn't you have just taken me to a fucking hotel?" I yelled and slammed the door in his face. I threw myself down on my office couch and screamed into my pillow.

Why had I said that stuff to the camera? Wolf's family's faces were swimming through my mind. Those sweet kids, the sound of Jillian's bold laughter, Drew and Lauren's caring nature, and Jim—that charming man who'd raised his kids into wonderful adults after tragically losing his love.

My heart plummeted. *What have I done?*

I heard Wolf's footsteps moving away from the door and what I assumed was him sitting in a chair. I heard him swear, and then Salone's voice saying, "Hey, Patty. Yeah, I need relief for Wolf and myself. Yeah, we have a little situation over here. Well, then what about Daniels and O'Dell? Yeah, I know it's not their job, but can you just ask them since they're on tonight and briefed already? Okay, great. I'll be talking with Commander Thompson about it tomorrow. Rivers and I won't be on this case. Yup. Thanks, Patty. Yeah, you, too. Goodnight." It was quiet again for a small while, and then I heard Salone lay into Wolf.

"What the actual fuck were you thinking? I get why you didn't tell me, but seriously, this is quite possibly the dumbest thing I think—no, I *know* you've ever done since I've known you. Jesus Christ, man! I know you're hurting after Tiffany, and the girl is gorgeous, but Jesus, Wolf! Jesus!"

"I don't want to hear it, Evelyn. And this had absolutely nothing to do with Tiffany." Wolf's voice sounded strained and tired.

Evelyn? The tough old broad had a name.

Wolf continued, "I can't even think straight right now. Do you really think it's such a good idea for me to be off this case? I mean, shit! I've already done so much digging into the Conners these past couple days, and I was considering asking Chief for my old position back so I can concentrate even more on it. I feel like if we focused, we may be able to pinpoint who might come for her next."

A laugh that held no humor, just disbelief came from Salone. "Pinpoint who? Are you crazy? You heard her out there! She invited not just the Conners but every sick, psycho, woman-hating, serial-killer rapist to come at her! The Conners are obviously a problem for her—and sounds like possibly your family now, too—but all the rest who will be coming for her… Rivers, there is no way to predict who is going to answer that call."

I had done that. I had invited every psychopath to come busting through my door. I must have looked crazy as shit spewing all that out, and the way things worked these days, I would be trending before long.

I didn't want Wolf's family in the middle of my mess. They were good people. I wasn't too concerned about Wolf because I was pretty positive he could take care of himself, and I doubted the Conners were dumb enough to go after a cop.

I wasn't concerned about myself either. I was too angry right now to feel scared. Too raw and ripped apart from what had happened to my baby. Whether someone was looking out for me, or it had been sheer dumb luck my little ass had taken down two big bad guys without much physical damage done, I didn't know. Could I keep up my track record? Doubtful. I had no actual fighting experience, very little muscle mass, and zero escape strategies for if someone successfully got their arms around me.

I curled onto my side on the couch, crying into the cushions. I didn't know if I was crying for myself, for Wolf's family, or for what I had said to Wolf. I knew I wasn't crying about the bastard that was now dead at my hands. I was still so angry. Partly because I knew the sound of his skull caving in on itself was going to haunt my dreams for the rest of my life. My stomach churned thinking about it, and I took deep breaths.

It wasn't until I heard a light knock on the door that I sat up, placing my bandaged hand in my other hand's palm. The numbing cream had worn off, and my hand was pulsating with pain, but it was secondary to the emotional pain I was feeling.

Wolf entered the room and shut the door. He leaned against it and looked at me. I could see there was a little anger still in his expression but mainly, what I saw in his face was regret.

My eyes were still streaming with tears. He sighed, and I knew he wanted to move toward me, but he didn't; he stayed right where he was.

I spoke before he could. "I'm sorry I said all that stuff. I should have thought things through. I was just so angry. If anything happens to your family… I just…I am so sorry, Wolf."

He didn't say anything for a while and then, "I'm going to convince them to go to my dad's lake house for a while until things blow over. You were right, I should have just taken you to a hotel."

Frustratingly, that stung. I knew I agreed, I had said the exact same thing moments before, but it didn't change the fact that what I was feeling now, with those words being uttered, was worse than how I had felt in a long time.

"I am sorry about Rosie. Goodbye, Raven." He turned, opened the door, and then he was gone. He'd left. It was better this way, I knew, but I still put my face in my hands and cried some more.

How did this happen? How did I go from pure bliss with him that very morning…to this? Or even only just a couple of hours before in the hospital, to feeling…whatever it was I was feeling about him.

Not much time passed before another body was in the room with me—Salone. She awkwardly patted my shoulder. "Detectives O'Dell and Daniels are here. They're going to take you to a hotel. Raven, I am really sorry for everything that happened to you, and for what it matters, I think you're one of the bravest young ladies I've ever met, albeit a little reckless. I hope you make it through all this okay. Remember, you have my number if you need me." She didn't wait for a response before she walked out.

When I didn't budge to leave, Daniels came in. He was a short, middle-aged man, handsome with kind-looking smile creases around his eyes and mouth. I imagined he was a dad with daughters. "Let me know what I can help you gather up," he offered.

I numbly walked around the house, grabbing my laptop and charger and my purse, then headed to my bedroom. Oddly enough, it didn't feel as daunting being in there as it had only hours before. Maybe the fact that multiple rooms in my house now held shared trauma somehow changed it. Or maybe it was that I was currently void of most emotion and so it just wasn't computing.

I was loading a bag full of clothes and toiletries when the thought occurred to me that I should probably have some sort of weapon. I didn't have Rocky's gun anymore, and there was no way I was swiping a knife from the kitchen with Detective O'Dell still casing the area. The man was nice enough, but of the two, he played the bad cop well while Daniels played good cop. A tall, solid man likely in his 40s, O'Dell would probably be good looking if his face was less serious.

I sighed as I surveyed my options. I had razor blades for shaving and a small pair of scissors in my makeup kit. Those would have to do for now. I clung to the hope that maybe my hotel room would prove more fruitful for a makeshift weapon or two.

"Let's go," I said to the two men and walked out my door, my tears now dried.

Chapter Twenty-Two

A few days later, the investigation closed. I decided to head back to my home. As per my request, O'Dell and Daniels had ensured that only officers they trusted moonlighted as my private security throughout my entire time at the hotel. The detectives themselves checked on me every day as well. But not a peep had come from Wolf. No call or text, just complete and utter silence from him, and it hurt, even as I tried to tell myself what happened between us had been nothing.

After getting settled in the hotel that first night after Rylan attacked, I had looked at the messages I'd missed earlier in the day from Wolf, while he had been at work, and I had been in my office. Rosie had been slumbering nearby, safe and content. The messages had been cute and flirtatious. In the final text, he'd asked me out to dinner and then to Devon's game the next night.

There had been an entire future that possibly could have been there. One I could see now—full of late-night binge sessions and nerding out together about the books we were reading, enjoying incredible meals, cheering for Devon at his games, watching Sara in her performance of *The Dancing Nutcracker*, and spending the Christmas holiday with a loving family.

And now…now I would never know what could have been. I would never have that chance. He wanted nothing to do with me, and even if he did, I could never let him be involved with me anymore. My life was about to get messy; probably very messy.

I had vehemently and continuously refused to go into hiding. However, the State Prosecutor's Office threatened to charge me with twelve counts of reckless endangerment regarding my neighbors.

Because of my ever-so-thoughtful invitation to potentially dangerous assailants, the stipulation was for me to list my house for sale in the next 30 days and make a statement that I was, in fact, no longer living there. Unfortunately, I had gone viral, and although most of the videos of my rant had been deleted from the web to protect my neighbors, the dark web was taking off with it.

In an attempt to convince me to go into hiding, right before leaving the hotel, Detective O'Dell explained there was a forum that had started up on the dark web regarding premeditated attacks on me. He was concerned about multiple different anonymous posters who were explicitly describing their plans.

"Raven, the amount of chatter on this forum is worrisome, to say the least."

I sat on the edge of the couch with my packed bag at my feet. "Can't you arrest them? I know they are anonymous, but with technology nowadays and tracing IP addresses, most of these people could be easily located, right?"

"It's not that simple."

"Why not? Isn't a threat a crime in the state of Wisconsin? If this forum is about me, and they are threatening me with what they intend to do, then couldn't I press charges?"

"Well, yes, but no one is going to pursue looking into who these people are—at least not anyone in my department, and I highly doubt BCSO would. The amount of resources it would take…you would have to hire someone yourself, and then the entire process of pressing charges would take some time. The charges wouldn't be worth it, is my point. It would involve other states and possibly other countries' jurisdiction, depending on where the posters are located. Plus, let's not forget that these technically aren't threats. You invited them to come at you. It could stand up in court that they were just answering your call and not actually threatening you at all."

"Then, why are you even telling me this if there is nothing we can do?" I almost shouted at him. If he wasn't going to help then he needed to stop wasting my time.

"Because I want you to be aware of what you might be stepping into if you go back to your home. Everyone on that forum knows your exact location. You will be getting visitors, and, I would expect, very soon. People you come in contact with could get hurt as well. Raven, you clearly have the means to move and go into hiding if you wanted, and I highly recommend that you do so and stay low on the radar for a while."

"I will move out of this state and never return," I said easily. "As soon as I find my dog. Until then, I'm not going to hide or run away."

O'Dell looked at me like I was insane. But after a moment, he nodded his head, "Alright then. I can drop you off at your house whenever you are ready. I'll be just outside." He stood up from the small desk in the room and exited. I sat on the uncomfortable couch a little longer before rising and gathering my things up.

I wasn't insane. It did terrify me that people were coming to attack me—that people were so obsessed with the thought they were writing about it. I wasn't going to go into hiding, but I would agree to list my home; it wasn't my neighbors' fault this all happened, and they deserved to feel safe in their homes.

My plan was to go back to California, but I wouldn't leave without knowing what happened to Rosie, and she hadn't been found. No remains or anything, as if she'd never existed at all. Sometimes, I let myself imagine Rylan hadn't been as cruel as his brother and had just let her outside, where she'd wandered off. Maybe someone found her, and she was in a warm home, safe and loved. Deep down, I doubted that was true. She was chipped, and any decent person who found a dog would check to see if there was someone out there looking for them. Still, I continued to keep a small kernel of hope and went out on multiple walks each day to different areas throughout Green Bay, and sometimes, I even had company.

That was one way my life had changed for the better since the attack from Rylan. I had reached out to all my neighbors to fervently apologize for everything I had said on live news and explained that I would be moving as soon as possible. The majority were warm, understanding, and sympathetic to my situation. However, none were more supportive than the two houses that sandwiched my own.

Shandra and her husband, Dale, put up home surveillance cameras outside their house to get multiple angles of my home in case someone acted upon my invite. My neighbors to the other side, young twin brother roommates, Jesse and Jake, helped me go through my house, putting up indoor and outdoor cameras and an alarm system. They even came up with a plan that I would text them each night before I went to bed and again when I woke up to ensure I was alive and well.

The level of support my neighbors had shown me was overwhelming to say the least—these were good people. I wanted to move out as soon as possible to keep anything bad from happening to them. These were people I was starting to trust—a scary thing for me to do, almost scarier than the attacks had been. Trusting others was something I reserved for those I loved, or people who'd proven their morality, like my old social worker, Brenda…and Wolf. My neighbors had shown me kindness over the past days that I wasn't sure I deserved, and so, I'd been meticulously packing up all my stuff from the moment I was back in my house.

"I can't believe we never talked before all this," Jesse said. We were on one of our walks in our neighborhood with his chocolate Lab, Cooper.

"Well, I can. I pretty much kept to myself on purpose. And you know it's not smart for me to be talking to you, now more than ever."

Jesse waved off my guilt as he and Jake had from the start. "No, no, it's fine. Look—you have the gun I gave you, right?"

"Yes. Well, not on me. It's at home," I confessed.

Jesse creased his eyes. He was 21 years old, bulky and average height, with a full, dark beard and bright brown eyes. "You should really carry it on your person. Also, if you want, I can get up to my parents' cabin and get some of the shotguns we have." The brothers were avid hunters, and although we were complete opposites in so many ways, they'd both taken me under their wings the past couple weeks. With some trips to the shooting range last week, I was sad to say I felt quite comfortable with a gun in my hand now; not like that first time I fired a gun—at Caleb, scared and unsure. And, judging by my second aim at Caleb, I was an excellent shot. I'd received better scores than both the brothers with nearly all the guns they'd had me try out.

I liked walking with Jesse and Cooper. It made me feel a little more normal, like how I had been before the Conners entered my life…like when Rosie and I would go on walks. I missed her so much. Too many times, I'd go to call her name or lean down to pet her.

And, if I was being honest with myself, I missed Wolf. I missed his voice and his arms around me. I missed being with him in his bed and hearing his heartbeat under my resting head. I missed his family, even though I had only met them a couple of times. It was a pointless, annoying thing—missing someone who didn't want you around. Missing someone you hadn't even spent that much time with. But I couldn't help it. I missed him.

"I mean, I have multiple knives and the one gun you gave me. If I can get more, at least while I'm still in this house, I will take what I can get. Thanks."

He smiled. "No problem. Jake and I will head out to the cabin tomorrow and get them."

We walked around a little while longer before heading back home, and parted ways with a reminder from him to text before bed.

The brothers had invited me to stay with them, to keep me safe. They didn't realize in their young minds that it was I that needed to keep them safe. Yes, they were both strong and fearless seeming individuals but they had no idea what I was up against. Heck, I wasn't even fully aware yet.

When I walked back into my house, I shrugged off my coat, scarf, and hat, placing them on the back of my couch. I paused, my hand still on my hat. Something felt off.

I looked around the room and then heard it. A light beeping sound. It took me a moment but I moved around the room until finally discovering that it was likely coming from my internet modem in my entertainment center.

I leaned down and opened the glass door. I froze. It was unplugged. In fact, it wasn't the modem at all making noise. It was the security system unit we'd installed that was beeping.

I deeply regretted not having that gun on my person. The alarm system and cameras were apparently no match for a seasoned invader.

I swiveled from my squatted position and stood quickly. He was maybe ten feet from me.

My heart stopped.

"Hellooo, Raven."

The stranger's voice was a sickening, sing-song tone which almost instantly had me begging for the Conners' creepy gruff voices instead.

He moved so quickly I didn't have time to grab the knife strapped to my thigh.

His hand grabbed my neck as he barreled into me, ramming me into the entertainment center and whacking my head hard against what only could have been the edge of my television. His other hand grabbed my wrist, keeping my right hand and arm immobile. I felt the warm wetness of blood from my head already drenching my hair.

He leaned in and whispered into my ear, "I came as fast as I could for you. Thanks for waiting." He turned around with his hand still gripping my throat and dragged me.

I fought with all my strength, which wasn't much, to grip something with my feet, legs, anything! My hands were grasping at his forearm and hand, scratching and clawing. The man laughed as he tore me from the room and pulled me into my bedroom, shoving me by the throat onto the bed like I was a rag doll—like I was nothing. But at least he'd released his hold on my neck.

I had come close to passing out, darkness creeping in, the pressure on my throat was too much. Unable to scream because I was too preoccupied slurping up air, I grabbed for the knife on my side, hoping he hadn't seen it, but as I reached down, my hand gripped nothing.

I sat up on my knees, holding my neck, still sucking in air. "Thanks for coming," I rasped out in between inhalations.

He smiled at me with my knife in his hand. It was a hideous smile with crooked yellow teeth going all different ways. His pale-gray eyes were the dead-looking sort under a mop of muted, ruddy-colored hair. He had to be around forty years old but looked much older, and he was tall and wiry. He threw the knife to the ground. "Won't be needing this." He jumped onto the bed, knocking me back.

Since coming home from the hotel, I had planted weapons—knives mostly, and the one gun that Jesse had given me—throughout the house. I cursed myself again for not carrying the gun on my person, but a knife should have been under both pillows on my bed. What if he'd cased the house before I had gotten home? Would the knives still be under my pillows? And if they were, would he find them first and use them against me? He didn't seem to want to use weapons, only his…hands. Those hands, which were currently unzipping his pants.

I didn't let the fear settle in long, though, and I prepared myself to get ahold of the knives by any means necessary.

When he launched himself on me the next second, I slipped my hands under each pillow, grasping for the knives. *They're still there!* I kicked my legs and bucked my thighs up, mostly to distract him. I grabbed each knife.

He squeezed my throat again with his right hand, and his desire was evident as he pressed against me. "Pretty girl. You're a very pretty girl. Pretty Pocahontas," he sing-songed.

My stomach turned. I wondered what he would do if I barfed right then and there in his face, and a desperate idea came to mind. Past the pressure he had on my throat, I screeched, "I'm going to puke!" He paused for a second, easing his hand. I took a quick breath and slid my hands as swiftly as I could out from under the pillows and slammed the knives into the first parts of him I could achieve contact with.

The knife in my right hand managed to stab right below his left shoulder blade. The knife in my left hand found the base of his neck, and I wrapped my legs around him, holding him close. His scream was a shriek I wouldn't ever forget, the sound piercing my eardrums.

His hands came down hard on my ribs. He punched my sides over and over as I tried to pull the knives back out but only managed to get one. He slammed his head down on mine, and the pain was so severe I almost blacked out, but his screaming kept me on my task, which was to take the one knife I'd dislodged from his body and slam it into his neck.

And I did. Again and again and again and again. I didn't stop until I was sure he wasn't moving, wasn't breathing, wasn't living.

His blood soaked me—my face, my neck, my body, and his dead weight pressed down on me. The pain in my sides was so excruciating, all thoughts of my throat and head vanished, and then the lights went out.

Chapter Twenty-Three

When I awoke, realizing I was in a hospital bed, Salone was at my side. Her eyes were wet with tears and my thoughts were frantic, wondering if something was wrong with Wolf. Why else would the old woman be crying?

"Raven?" she searched my eyes and then clicked a button near the bed. A nurse came in shortly after and then a doctor. I was asked questions yet told to not speak, and that made no sense at all. I tried to anyway, only to find my throat felt like it was on fire. It was explained that I'd suffered trauma to my neck, three broken ribs, a concussion, and a gash in my scalp that received stitches. I felt each pain as they spoke of them.

Soon, it was just Salone with me in the small room. "Raven, his name was Salvador Scholl. He was a serial rapist. He—he's raped seven women and was wanted in three states." She grabbed my arm softly, avoiding all the tubes coming out of them. "You ended all of that. He won't ever inflict pain or suffering on another woman ever again…because of you."

Tears flowed from me. Tears of happiness? Relief? I wasn't sure. My invite to the world of criminals and attackers may have been reckless, but this was something incredible I hadn't considered—it also was saving people from harm.

Salone's eyes shone as she released my arm. "Thank you. Thank you for fighting. Thank you for staying strong. Get some rest now. You'll be safe here." I nodded slightly, and my eyes slowly closed.

When I woke again, I knew without even opening my eyes that the hand encircling my own was Wolf's. In fact, I refused to open my eyes, because I knew I'd have to deal with reality, and I was just so tired of that lately. What I would give to go back to that morning of pretending. But I eventually did open my eyes, because part of me wanted to see the beautiful man beside me.

"Raven?" his tired voice reached out. He sat up straighter, his other hand now softly on my shoulder. The hand holding mine tightened, his thumb dragging circles around and around my knuckles. He was anxious.

"Wolf." I spoke, but my voice was all wrong and it hurt. It hurt so much to speak. I moved my hand instinctively up to my throat, only to be reminded my arm was full of tubes.

"Please don't speak if it hurts."

So, I didn't, I just nodded with tears in my eyes. He turned the TV on, and we watched old episodes of *Friends* before I dozed off again.

I woke up just as a nurse was letting Wolf know that visiting hours were over. He agreed he would be leaving soon, and she left the room for us to say our goodbyes.

We looked at each other for a moment before he dropped his head to mine. No words needed. He knew I was sorry for the things I said the other week. I knew he was sorry for how he dealt with it as well.

Finally he sighed and leaned up.

"You'll have an officer outside your room for the remainder of your care here, and they aren't moonlighting. The FBI is in talks with our department and BCSO. The FBI, Raven! That's how serious this just got!"

I just stared at him—at his worried, beautiful face.

"Are you done with this now? Will you please go into hiding? Or…or I can take you somewhere. We can go to Mexico or Canada or anywhere. Literally anywhere. New Zealand and rent out a Hobbit house for fuck's sake. I'll take you anywhere." His eyes were burning into me, wishing me to agree with him, the blue of them giving off an aqua hue from the hospital's fluorescent lighting.

But I couldn't do what he asked. I wouldn't. Not after what Salone had told me. Not after finding out I had saved people.

So even though it hurt to speak, I told him, "I can't, Wolf. I won't."

Wolf's hand left mine and he stood, pacing in front of the bed. "*Why*, Raven? *Why* do you intend to punish yourself like this? You made a mistake saying what you said. I care about you, and I know you care about me. And, yeah, so we haven't known each other long, but I don't care about that. We can go away from here, and…" his voice trailed off, realizing it was useless. We both knew he couldn't leave his family, his job.

I took a slow breath. "I won't run away from my problems, Wolf, and I won't allow you or your family to be a part of them. Please…leave me alone." My heart hurt uttering those words. The one thing in the world I had wanted, from the moment I met him, was for him to not leave me alone. It was all that had mattered. The one thing that made sense.

He didn't move for a long time, but then he found his voice. "Is that really what you want?" His eyes bore into mine, looking, searching for something I wouldn't give him.

"Yes," I said easily, because it was. Because I did care about him, and I didn't want him to get hurt. Because everybody I'd ever truly cared about died, and I was done with that.

The hurt and yet the understanding that was distinct on his face made me want to cry. "Okay," he said, and he headed toward the door.

A flurry of thoughts hit me fast and all at once. I stopped him as he approached the threshold. "Wait. Wolf? Will you do me a favor?"

Wolf turned, his eyes shining. "Of course."

I exhaled softly as my throat felt like it was closing in on itself. "I have family." He took a step forward then, clearly shocked. "I have family on the Rain Tree Reservation. My birth mother's family; the Winters. Good people. Beautiful, wonderful people. That's why I came to Wisconsin. It's a long story…" I trailed off. "Can you just make sure nobody is able to find out they are related to me? The creeps coming for me, the Conners. If they knew... Just, please."

He could tell I couldn't talk anymore, and he moved to me, softly placing his hand on my arm. "I will do everything I can to make sure they are safe. I promise. And I will never stop looking for Rosie."

Tears slipped down my eyes at the mention of my Rosie girl. She had deserved so much more, and my heart ached at the thought. "Thank you. And if you do find her, please take her to the Winters. She'll be safe there."

He wiped my tears with his thumb, a caress I moved my head into. Then he turned and walked out of the room, but I said one last thing: "I do care about you."

I wasn't sure if he heard me or not, because he didn't look back.

Chapter Twenty-Four

After a couple more days of being in the hospital, I was finally going to be discharged. I had given multiple statements to the police regarding what had occurred. There was no reason for them not to believe me at this point, but I would not be going back to my home. I'd made arrangements from the hospital to have my bed thrown out—there was no way I could stomach seeing that again—and my things boxed up and put in storage. I would not go back in that house; I couldn't put my neighbors at risk again.

Detective O'Dell came into the hospital room as I was getting ready to leave. The pain in my throat and ribs had considerably lessened but were still constantly aching, as I had refused the hard medicine they were prescribing me. Even so, the doctors and nurses were very happy with my progress.

"Raven, before we go, I want you to talk with someone. You okay with that?" O'Dell asked.

I sat down tenderly on the hospital bed. "Who?"

"His name is Brock, and I'd like you to just hear him out."

I nodded. Was this another therapist of sorts? Two had already checked in on me while I had been in the hospital, so what did I care if one more wanted to chat? I had always gotten something out of therapy sessions, so it couldn't hurt; Brenda had me go to them as a young child and again after losing Lilly.

O'Dell left the room and returned less than a minute later. A massive man with a military-style haircut followed O'Dell into the room. He was probably only a few inches taller than me, but that massiveness didn't come from his height, it came from his stocky, muscular build. His brown eyes were intense as they assessed me. He came over and sat in a chair in front of me, his hands clasping on his lap.

O'Dell closed the door. "Raven, this is Brock. He is the owner and trainer of a self-defense and mixed martial arts facility here in the city."

Okay, so not a therapist. I looked from O'Dell to Brock, who was staring intently at me.

"Hi, Raven. Detective O'Dell has briefed me on the situation you have found yourself in. Before I go any further, I need to ask you one question: Do you feel that any sort of self-defense or training would be beneficial to you?"

Of course it would be. Did I have any real passion or desire to learn how to fight? No. No, not at all. But I did have a desire to live and to never feel as helpless as I had when Salvador had dragged me by the throat and threw me on that bed. "Yes. I know it would be."

Brock simply nodded. "Good. Good. And am I correct in that you do not want to go into hiding?"

"Yes, you are correct. That can't happen."

"Well, if you agree to what I have to offer, you will be going off the grid." He held up his hand as I was about to protest. "Hear me out. It won't be hiding, and it won't be running. You need time to heal, and you need time to train. You won't be able to take down any more of those sick fucks if you wind up dead because of your lack of skill set and strength." The way he spoke of my future assailants had me mentally straightening up, and I surmised that he had experienced loss at the hands of people of that sort.

"You will be off the grid just for as long as I deem necessary. Then you'll be back out there, fighting the bad guys."

"Why would you do this for me? What's the catch?"

O'Dell spoke up. "There's no catch. He's doing me a favor. And Raven, so you know, if you agree to this, nobody but the three of us in this room and those Brock brings in to train with you will know about it. Not Captain Riv—I mean, Officer Rivers or Salone, not even the Commander of the Green Bay Police. You will not be able to have any outside contacts."

Luckily for me, I wasn't a social butterfly. I would need to at least let my neighbors know I wouldn't be reachable and to not worry. I glanced at the flowers and cards several of my neighbors had brought in and the balloon from Jake. "I can do that, but then who will be training with me?" I looked to Brock.

"I have people who can be trusted not to speak," he said.

People *he* trusted…but would I? Did I even trust him? Or O'Dell, for that matter? I didn't have the luxury of time to build that sense of trust, though. What was my gut saying? Brock was too new; I couldn't get a read on him. But O'Dell…yes, I believed I trusted O'Dell. I knew Wolf did.

It was evident Brock wasn't going to give me details on the people he would involve. That was fine. I supposed I would learn soon enough who they were.

"This is how it will go down. Detective O'Dell is going to persuade the hospital to give you one more day here. You will use that time to get your affairs in order. Whatever that is—your job, family, and friends. Your house, your car, pets, whatever. Get it all figured out, because when I come tomorrow, you'll be leaving with me, and we'll be going straight to the facility. I have a back entrance with a private training area and a small apartment where you and those I bring in will be staying for the duration of your training. There will be no outside technology."

I took a shaky breath. Shit just got really serious. I was being offered something that I couldn't turn down, but I was nervous, to say the least.

Worth it. It will be worth it.

"What if the authorities need to get ahold of me?" I looked to O'Dell. "What if the Conners get antsy when they're not able to find me and press charges as a way to bring me out?"

O'Dell adjusted his stance near the door. "I will take care of that. Commander Thompson doesn't know the specifics here with Brock, but Raven, the FBI and Thompson approved that I put something in place for you and that I would be your only outside point of contact for the duration of it. I will reach out to Brock if there is anything that warrants your knowledge or presence, and he will get us in contact."

I was quiet then, thinking. Two agents from the FBI had come to talk to me a couple of days before. Apparently, the dark web forum O'Dell had told me about was blowing up, and they believed there were a few extremely wanted individuals behind some of the posts.

Was I being used by the FBI to take out bad guys, and they weren't even going to tell me? They'd just agreed with the Commander of the Green Bay Police to have O'Dell put something in place? But I had brought this upon myself; not the first couple Conner attacks, but Salvador and the rest that were coming. Regardless, whether I took Brock up on his offer to train me or not, those attacks were not going away. At least this way I would receive training and have a real fighting chance.

"I'll do it," I finally said. "I'll go off-grid with you and accept your training."

I reached my hand out and Brock stood up and shook it.

"Thank you. I don't know how I'll ever be able to repay you," I told him.

He released my hand but I felt his hold still on me. The man packed a seriously intense presence. "You can repay me by stopping all those bastards that come at you." He walked to the door and stood by O'Dell. "Tell Detective O'Dell your sizes for shoes and clothing, and I'll have gear and training clothes ready to go. I'll be back to get you tomorrow morning." He nodded once and then was gone.

O'Dell didn't have a problem persuading hospital staff to allow me one more day. Daniels came to check on me, but not before O'Dell reminded me to not mention anything about where I was going. Daniels didn't ask, and I suspected he knew not to.

I spent the entire day tying up loose ends with work, taking my website down, and sending refunds and apologies to those who had placed orders over the past week that I would not be able to fill. I called Shandra and asked her to have my car put in storage.

I called Jesse where I learned that he and Jake were the ones who found me. Jake had come to check on me because I hadn't sent my usual bedtime check-in text. When I didn't answer my door, Jake had gone back to get Jesse. They busted the door open and called the cops when they'd seen the bloody scene; sure that I was dead. Although, I felt horrible having to ask them to go back to the scene of the crime, I did. They were going to do a walk-through of my house after the movers left and get the information I would need for the storage.

Last, I called my realtor to check on how the process was going. There hadn't been any offers. Technically, I was moved out of the house, and it was listed for sale, which was what the State Prosecutor's Office wanted to see. I wouldn't be there any longer.

If anything, the past few weeks had shown me that as much as I didn't want to care about people and as much as I wanted to be a loner, I needed people. People need people in this world. And at that moment, all I had or would allow myself to have were the relationships with my neighbors who had stood by me the past couple weeks, O'Dell, and now Brock and his crew. Whoever they might be.

Chapter Twenty-Five

The next morning, I gave my phone and laptop to O'Dell. He handed me a duffle bag of clean clothes and toiletries, and when he left, Brock appeared in the doorway. He passed me a green jacket with a hood and a black beanie. He grabbed my face in his beefy hands before I could protest and rubbed a colored stick across my eyebrows. I was so stunned I didn't even stop him.

"This is to turn your eyebrows red. Your medical mask will cover most of your face, but it's likely that multiple people are waiting to see you come out of the hospital, and we can't let them know where you're going. O'Dell is about to depart with a female officer out of uniform who will be a decoy, and you and I will leave shortly thereafter."

He shoved a walking boot on my uninjured foot and handed me crutches. "You will be another patient leaving the hospital for all anyone is concerned." He chucked a tan scarf at me and took his jacket off, flipping it inside out. The black jacket was now orange. He grabbed a green beanie out of the pocket and placed it on his head as he adjusted his own medical mask.

"I have the feeling you've done this type of thing a time or two," I said. Bundled now in a scarf and multiple layers, it was probably hard to discern if I was a preteen boy or a shorter female.

He grunted in response. "Let's go."

We walked out of the hospital and into the frigid air. I thought it might be nice for my training to last at least throughout the winter months, so I wouldn't have to deal with the snowy season; last year's winter had been a real shock to my California soul.

Brock put the crutches in the back seat and helped me into the passenger side of a gray Toyota sedan. It was completely un-eye-catching.

When Brock got into the driver's seat, he looked at me. "I want you to understand that over the next few weeks, you are going to be put in some very uncomfortable situations. I will break you down to build you back up. I'm not doing it to be cruel. I am doing it because I want you to be prepared for anything as much as you can be. There will be times when you are going to hate me or my men. Know that we have your best interest in mind."

I scoffed at him. "You couldn't have told me all this before I made my decision yesterday?"

"Would your decision have changed if I had?"

I thought for a moment and then replied, "No." I needed to be put in uncomfortable scenarios I supposed. But, surely, he would let me fully recover before training got too intense.

We drove aimlessly for an hour to ensure we weren't being followed. By the time we finally arrived in front of a large building, I had almost dozed off multiple times.

It was plain and white with chipped paint and a blue stripe painted around the entire building. The name on the building read *Alpha Dog Training and Self-Defense*. Well, that was cute—and by cute, I meant it sounded ridiculous.

There was no one on the sidewalks as he helped me out of the car, led me to the back of the building, down a cement staircase, and unlocked a back door. I still had the crutches and boot on as I made my way into the dark room. Brock entered behind me and slammed the door shut, locking it.

"Is there a light switch or something?" I moved to turn toward the wall when the next thing I knew, Brock ripped the crutches from me and shoved me down to the ground. A light flipped on, bright and temporarily blinding me.

Lying on the ground, my chest heaving and my sides stinging with pain, my mind reeled with the recent traumas I had faced.

I eventually managed to get on my hands and knees and glared back at Brock. When his face finally came into view, it revealed no remorse.

He stared back at me and said, "Have at her, men."

I turned my head to see three figures emerge from their hiding places, approaching me simultaneously from different sides of the room.

So much for fully recovering first; my training had apparently begun.

DID YOU ENJOY THIS BOOK?

Then you'll definitely enjoy the second book in the series!
The next in the Come And Get Me series, *The Warrior*, will be available 2026!
Keep up to date with Shay Therese's upcoming novels by connecting to any of the following:
www.shaytherese.com

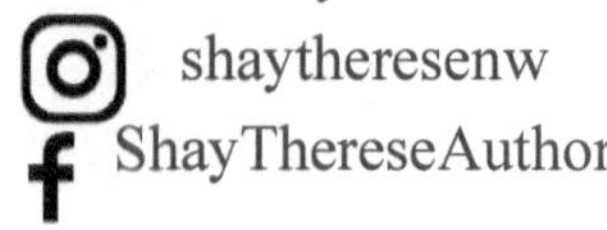

shaytheresenw
ShayThereseAuthor

Author's Note on the Rain Tree Tribe

After a long internal debate, it was my decision to use a fictitious tribe located in Wisconsin. At the time of writing this novel, the state of Wisconsin has eleven federally recognized tribes and one still seeking recognition; Bad River Band of the Lake Superior Tribe of Chippewa Indians, Brothertown Indian Nation, Forest County Potawatomi Community, Ho-Chunk Nation, Lac Courte Oreilles Band of Lake Superior Chippewa, Lac du Flambeau Band of Lake Superior Chippewa, Menominee Nation, Oneida Tribe of Indians of Wisconsin, Red Cliff Band of Lake Superior Chippewa, St. Croix Chippewa Indians of Wisconsin, Sokaogon Chippewa Community, and Stockbridge-Munsee Band of Mohican Indians. I point this out because as a member of a tribal community in the Pacific Northwest, I was uncomfortable writing about another tribe's culture, as all indigenous communities throughout the United States of America and Canada are unique. Each tribe also has had a different relationship with the federal government. Other books in this series will visit the Rain Tree Reservation, and I wanted to be respectful of the Wisconsin tribal communities in not getting any details wrong regarding their history or way of life. This is why I ultimately came to the decision to not use one of the tribes listed above for the Winters family.